Black Light

A Novel by
Galway Kinnell

North Point Press
San Francisco
1980

Observe the so-called 'half-moon'. The half of it that faces the day is dressed in borrowed light. The half of it that faces the night is dressed in its own light. The same with a simple lamp. Down low, the flame is white. Halfway up, it already begins changing itself into black smoke.

—*Sohrawardi*

Chapter One

Jamshid kept sliding forward as he worked, so that the patch of sunlight would remain just ahead of him, lighting up the motion of his hands. He was restoring the head of a bird of paradise, where a lump of charcoal had burnt its way through. As he always did when it was a question of a gap through which darkness was visible, he was working with nervous speed. He valued for more than its light this trapezoid of sunlight that glided beside him over the flowers and tendrils of his own carpet on the floor; it itself was like a carpet, but one that came from heaven.

He finished weaving in the bird's head, and he breathed more easily. Tomorrow morning he would seal closed the neck and breast, and then this gap too, like so many others, would be healed for good. The sun patch, touching the base of the wall, now started to diverge upward. Soon it would creep over the border of the geometrical and turn into chaos. This was the sign it was time to close shop.

Getting to his feet Jamshid saw the bird's head blur as it sank away from him. Closely as he had made it conform to the other heads on the carpet, it suddenly seemed peculiarly unreal, as if he had woven only the absence of a head. He felt a strange dread. In the last few weeks there had been other moments when a thing, when he glanced at it, would blur and become a dark tear in reality. But now the tear closed again as quickly as it had opened.

He hung the pomegranate-rind red and walnut-husk brown wools back in their places on a wall entirely covered in colored wools. These clumps of wool all had the same formless bulk and the same spongy substance. Their colors alone held them apart, as if the sun patch on the floor, diffracting upward, had cast a spectrum of more intense reality on this dead matter. Jamshid took the carpet he was repairing over to the west wall, where the sun patch would light it up in the morning. He swept up the trimmed-off bits of wool. He picked up the trimming shears and placed them on the table. He put on his trousers and jacket over his pajamas and stepped into his cotton-soled geevays. He drew the blind: smeared sunlight vanished and the clumps of wool went drab. It was Jamshid's own, punctual sunset.

His practice at this time of day was to go to the mosque and try to nap until the general sunset took place. His shop was at the north end of the bazaar and the nearest mosque was the Masjideh Jomeh. But Jamshid did not like this mosque, for it was in bad repair, and he hated seeing, where tiles and stalactites had fallen out, the wrinkled mud walls and convoluted plaster. He would go, instead, to the Masjideh Shah in the Shrine of the Immam Reza, even though to get there he had to pass through the entire bazaar, whose gloom, noise, filth, and commerce he hated.

Today, he felt particularly upset, and he made himself think of the harmonious mass of minarets and domes toward which he was going, azure and lapis lazuli, decorated all around with hieratic calligraphy and consummated by the golden dome that shed an essential light over its precincts. As he pushed through the suffocating maze, already dark, clogged with burdened men crying "Out of the way!" with donkeys, with bicycles jingling their little gasping doorbells, the passage seemed to Jamshid an ordeal to which he submitted only for the most ardent love of God.

He broke from the crowd and came out into the courtyard of the mosque. He stood reaccustoming himself to his element. In this rectangular space he felt something of the ordered calm on which he had just turned the key back at his shop. Many persons were gathered here, it was true, but the place had a way of diminishing them and of throwing their voices upward.

At the pool Jamshid washed his right hand, his left hand, his right foot, his left foot, his face and his teeth. He passed a dripping hand through his hair, from the brow to the back of the neck. As he stood up, he saw in the ripples an image of himself, and even though he shut his eyes he could not keep from seeing himself torn to pieces.

He lay down, but he found he was unable to sleep. Long ago, during the little interval between his wedding and his wife's death, he would lie awake under the stars a long time. Not until he had come to see that the stars were strung out in actual patterns had he become able to sleep. Recently, a new insomnia had returned. Now, he tried to empty his mind, but it was like looking into an empty sky and gradually seeing it was crawling with vultures. With relief he welcomed mundane worries back into his consciousness. If he was not going to sleep, he would at least think about something interesting in the attempt. Accordingly, he began fretting about his daughter. But soon he became aware of two persons talking to each other only a few feet away.

"Only for one week," the man was saying in a Kurdish accent.

"Then I need a settlement of one hundred tomans. Not a rial less." The woman spoke in the Shirazi accent, which is so lyrical when spoken by young women. Jamshid understood at once the nature of the transaction. He himself had once been mistaken for a pilgrim. A chaddor-clad woman had approached him in the courtyard and proposed to temporary-marry him. Though he tried not to notice them, at pilgrimage time one could see little discussions of this nature taking place in the vicinity of the Shrine. The pilgrims from distant cities and from Afghanistan and the Arab countries liked getting married for the few weeks of their sojourn, it helped to ease the spiritual rigors of the pilgrimage. The man laughed.

"In my country we say 'year' not 'week' when we mean all four seasons. One hundred tomans is fair settlement for a marriage lasting spring, summer, fall, and winter. But for a marriage lasting seven days, twenty tomans is all you will get! Not a rial more! And it's only your outrageous charm that makes me offer so much . . ." Jamshid lay still. As the two went on bargaining, a powerful rage came over him.

"And which mullah asks the least to perform the ceremony?" the Kurd asked.

"Torbati," the woman answered. "Everybody goes to Torbati, he's the most experienced, the quickest . . ."

Jamshid sat up. "Torbati!" he said aloud. It was like spitting. The man and the woman, startled, moved off. "Am I to trust the marriage of my only daughter to a mullah who is everybody's procurer?" The moazzin in the minaret lifted his nasal call to prayer. The last sparkle of sunlight fell from the golden dome. At any moment Mullah Torbati would be making his appearance to lead the prayer. Jamshid walked to where he had left his geevays and stepped into them.

"Furthermore, why should I let myself be led in prayer by the scoundrel?"

Chapter Two

Jamshid was one of the most pious men in the region, and he knew it. Yet, judging by the disrespectful way people treated him, one might suppose he was an infidel. He did feel a little ashamed that he had never made a pilgrimage to Mecca or for that matter to the Shrine of Fatima at Qum. But travel was expensive, and poverty was the price he paid for being honest. Other men cheated and grew rich, and then went on pilgrimages that consisted of sightseeing, good meals, and temporary marriages. When these travelers came home, they were called 'Haji', wore the green sash around their swollen bellies, and had only contempt for skinny and honest men like himself. Human sin—particularly among religious men—filled Jamshid with revulsion. Sometimes at prayer the feeling of revulsion grew so strong he could not concentrate on God at all. It was as if his virtue, his very devotion to God, were succeeding where vice had failed, in making an atheist out of him.

A man and woman were walking ahead of him. He thought he recognized them as the two persons he had overheard haggling in the mosque. The woman was cloaked in a chaddor and the man was wearing a darvish skullcap. Jamshid walked faster. Was their sudden appearance some sort of sign? Had God picked him, Jamshid, to follow and be their witness? As he came up behind them he could feel his heart beating with excitement. But the man turned his head and

Jamshid saw he was not the Kurd at all, but only a local darvish who repaired shoes in the bazaar.

"Salaam alaikum, Jamshid," the darvish said, "Not at your devotions tonight?" Jamshid noted the sarcasm in the man's tone.

"Salaam alaikum," he answered. "Will you kindly mind your own affairs?" He had intended to take the long way home and arrive at the usual hour, so that his daughter Leyla would not know he had skipped the sundown prayer. It could only do harm to a young girl to see her father give up ancient practices, no matter how justifiably. But to escape this busybody Jamshid had to turn down the first street he saw, which was a street that led directly home.

He heard a droshky behind him. It was moving only a little faster than he was, and it took a long time for it to overtake him. As it did, he turned his head. An old man sat in the high seat beating the old horse. A horse which apparently had discovered that to walk fast or to walk slow did not much affect the beating it got. The droshky seemed to be empty. At last it pulled ahead, shakily bearing away its little scene of harshness and indifference. It stirred some compassion within Jamshid—a compassion, he understood, for himself.

By the time he reached his house he was beginning to regret that he had not said his prayers. When you snap a single thread, he reflected, you threaten the whole fabric. He wondered if he shouldn't pray in his own garden. Or perhaps right here in the street. Or perhaps not at all, for a prayer said alone, he recalled, is twenty-seven degrees inferior to a prayer said in congregation. As he hesitated, the gate swung open. There stood Leyla and, close beside her, Akhbar the mason who had come that morning to repair the oven.

"Salaam alaikum," the mason said.

"Salaam alaikum, papa," Leyla said.

"Your oven is finished," said the mason. "I am just leaving."

"I can see," Jamshid answered. He entered the garden and walked over to the little brick oven that stood in one corner. Akhbar followed.

"It is better than when it was new," he said.

"You didn't waste your cement, I'll say that," said Jamshid, though in the dusk he could hardly see anything at all.

"Didn't waste my cement?" Akhbar replied. "What do you mean? I wasted a full kilo. Look, I put some around in back where the bricks were coming loose. Catch any other mason putting cement back there where nobody is ever likely to look. I even borrowed an extra handful from my father, which I wasn't planning to charge you for unless he notices it's gone."

"If you have wasted, as you say, a full kilo of cement, you have been eating it. How is it, by the way, that it took you a whole day to repair a tiny oven? I should be cursed by my ancestors for hiring the slowest mason in Meshed." Jamshid was talking almost automatically. He stopped short, as he remembered the haggling in the mosque.

"I have worked from morning to just now on this difficult oven," Akhbar was saying. "You see how queerly the thing is built, not a first-rate oven at all. But I have made it as good as new, if not considerably better . . ." Jamshid had stopped listening.

"Come to my shop tomorrow, we will settle matters then."

When Akhbar had left, Jamshid knelt by the pool. Though the water in it was cleaner, certainly, than that of the mosque pool, it felt unpleasant to wash for prayer in it. For that purpose one needs mosque water. Then, spreading his carpet in the direction of Mecca, he offered his evening prayers.

Dinner passed in silence. When Leyla was not serving him, she was standing off to one side. It seemed to Jamshid the rice was a bit too hard tonight and the curd-water just slightly too thin. He would tell her about it in the morning, when they did their accounts. After dinner had been cleared, Leyla brought him his waterpipe, on which she had already set the burning coals. He liked sitting on his carpet in the garden, drawing up the drenched smoke. It was nice, too, to hear the regular bubbling of the pipe, and to see the high, angular walls of the garden around the starry sky.

Jamshid shivered a little. The night air was cool. He felt like talking to his daughter. She would be eating in the kitchen. Should he mention the rice now, while she could see what he meant? He knew he had to prepare her to be a wife, and he congratulated himself that he was succeeding. She could cook well. She was quiet and obedient. She was in good health. She was pretty. With those virtues it was strange that, although she was sixteen, she had received not only no offers from suitors, but no inquiries either. Jamshid had brought up the matter with Mullah Torbati, who knew about such matters. He had heard of several advantageous marriages this mullah had arranged for girls with far fewer claims than Leyla. His discovery tonight that Torbati also specialized in temporary marriages had come as a shock to Jamshid. He would drop the mullah and find a husband for his daughter himself. Even if he had to go so far as to marry her to the son of Fereydoon the beet seller! He puffed angrily at his pipe. Leyla looked from the door.

"Papa, you sound like a lion."

"Leyla," Jamshid said, "did Akhbar really work hard all day, as he told me, or was he lolling around in the shade a good part of the time?" Leyla looked at him, he thought, a little oddly. Was there some trace of defiance, even contempt in her gaze? She dropped her eyes.

"Yes, father." Her voice was meek. "I did not watch him especially, but when unavoidably I happened into the garden I could not help noticing that he was always hard at work." She is a good girl, thought Jamshid, she loves and respects her father and does credit to the memory of her mother. It should not be hard to find her a suitable husband.

"Good," he said, and unrolled the bed clothes she had brought out for him. As he lay trying to sleep it struck him that Leyla had not inquired why he had said tonight's prayer at home. It irked him that, as far as he could tell, she hadn't even noticed. He looked up at the stars and cursed the neighbors, as he did every night, for growing that tree which, showing above the top of the wall, impinged on his rectangle of heaven.

Chapter Three

The next morning Jamshid knotted in the colors on the bird's neck and breast. He felt upset. He had slept only fitfully the night before, and he had had nightmares of this bird. In one nightmare the bird had changed into a vulture and had begun devouring the corpse of Leyla. In another it had swooped down on him extending its red beak, which changed into the mullah's henna-stained right hand, which then struck him. In another, its eyes contained hints of defiance and contempt, as they lowered in attitudes of perfect modesty.

Now, lighted by the trapezium of sunlight, it was the same bird as yesterday, once again belonging to paradise. But still from time to time he paused and stared at it and felt a strange dread, as if he were observing a snowflake just fallen on his warm palm. He knotted the knots very tightly, so that the bird would never fly again.

"Bird of Paradise . . ." he muttered, "Bird of Paradise . . ." He did not know why he said this. The bird did not hear.

By late morning Jamshid had finished weaving in the bird's neck and breast. He had knotted in all the colors and had clipped the wool ends smooth. His sense of discomfort had gone. The sun patch touched the center of the floor and was on the verge of becoming a perfect square. Jamshid dressed. At any minute the moazzin would begin calling the faithful to the noon prayer.

Mullah Torbati walked in the door.

"Salaam alaikum, Jamshid," the mullah said. Jamshid's eyes went at once to the mullah's henna-stained fingernails. The hand seemed to blur, as if a red beak were about to take shape. He looked back to the mullah's face.

"Salaam alaikum, Mullah Torbati," Jamshid said. A wave of revulsion surged up in him, but he resolved to hold his peace until he was more in control of himself.

"I have come to speak with you," the mullah said, "of your daughter." His voice was high-pitched and rasping, and he spoke with grave, insinuating authority.

"Ah, my daughter . . ." Jamshid mumbled.

"You asked me to occupy myself over your daughter, dosh Jamshid." The mullah called him by the slang for brother used between underworld fraternals. "I, who give myself in the service of God, am asked by a lowly repairer of rugs to find a match for his daughter. Mind you, I accept to do this. But to be truthful I have to tell you it is a difficult case . . . a *very* difficult case . . ." He paused to let his words seep in. Jamshid began to tremble.

"*Very* difficult . . ." the man of God continued. "A case my conscience had, yes, a scruple or two about accepting, a case only my devotion to good works and my friendly feelings toward you, brother Jamshid, finally persuaded me to undertake . . ." Now a placating tone came into the rasp. "A little extra contribution from you to the crippled and the poor . . ." he gestured deprecatingly, "could make all the difference . . . I might then, God willing, locate a candidate, pious, hardworking . . ."

"*Very?* . . ." said Jamshid.

The mullah's face lit up in a hideous smile. "Eh, brother Jamshid, so you know all about it?" The mullah stepped forward and his smile grew worse. Jamshid stepped back against the table. The sunpatch was absolutely perfect now. On the other side of it the black-robed, pale-headed figure shimmered like a bird. The voice rasped on. Jamshid could hardly make out what it was saying. "Of course you do. Who doesn't? I myself have tried, naturally, to ignore the ugly stories. Young men, after all, boast and invent, I know that. Nevertheless, nothing makes it harder to marry off a girl than a bit of gossip, even if not one word be true . . ." The mullah's expression now changed. His voice grew suddenly solicitous. "Ah, dosh, I see I have upset you." He stepped forward again, his arm extended. The red-beaked hand lit up as it entered the falling sunlight. "Oh, mind you, the case isn't hopeless, not at all," Torbati continued, with soothing unction in his tone. "You have me as your friend. I shall not allow them to slander the girl. Why just last night, in the coffee house, I shut up an ignorant dog of a mason . . ."

The hand opened suddenly as if it had caught fire. Jamshid took up the shears, stepped forward, and drove them with all his force into the mullah's breast. The mullah staggered, then fell backwards. He fell on his back in the sunpatch, which at once stretched grotesquely out of shape. The shears had gone in up to the hilt, and the handles protruded like a bow-knot tied on the breast bone.

Jamshid squatted down and looked at the body. He still saw the mullah alive. He saw his head turned to one side, nodding a little, as it did whenever the holy man mouthed sage advice. He could not help seeing the mullah as a little boy lying by the side of a pool. A nightingale was perched on the boy's breast, singing of the life in paradise. The pool of the man's blood touched Jamshid's foot, and he got up with a start. The sunlight had been inching forward and had already started to leave the corpse. He tried to think what he must do. It was clear, he must turn himself in. He felt glad that, unlike the mosque, the police station could be reached without going through the bazaar. In case they wanted to reconstruct the crime, he would, of course, leave everything exactly as it was. He stepped across the corpse, stumbling a little on it, as he went for the door.

At the door he stopped. Supposing they did not believe him and turned him away with scoffing laughter? He would have to make everything plain. Returning to the body, he took hold of the shears. By opening and shutting them slightly, making little silent snips down in the dead heart, he was able to loosen them. He went out with the shears in his hand. At the turning of the stairs someone was climbing. He saw the face of Akhbar the mason.

"Salaam alaikum," said Akhbar. "I have come to present my bill." Jamshid held out the shears, so as to indicate he could not discuss the bill at this moment. Having just come in from the sunlight, Akhbar did not see well and reaching to shake hands, he touched the shears.

"What the devil . . .?" he whispered.

"Now that bill . . ." said Jamshid, momentarily con-

fused. "Oh, yes, for the little oven? A graceful little thing
. . . meek . . . a good cook . . ." Akhbar had vanished
down the stairs.

A moment later Jamshid went back into the shop.
This time he fetched the black umbrella from the corner and dropped the shears into it. He saw that the
patch of sunlight had slipped almost entirely off the
body and was taking on its old geometrical form
again. There was something pleasing about that. The
body was turning drab.

Out in the street Jamshid could hear the loudspeak-
er in some minaret singing the call to prayer. It seemed
a piece of good luck that he had to go to the police station, and so did not have to go to these prayers, which
now seemed completely pointless. He registered the
extra weight of his umbrella. Mullah Torbati, for one,
he reflected, would not be at noon prayer either.

Chapter Four

Jamshid walked through the bright sunshine. From time to time he gave a little swing to the umbrella. School had just let out for the lunch hour and there were many children about. As a rule Jamshid did not care for children; he particularly disliked thinking of them in school, which he believed was bad for them. But now he experienced an almost giddy sympathy with these creatures who ran so freely in the sunlight. One little boy had a little girl down and was pummelling her. Jamshid, who another day might have beat them apart, merely looked on. Pretty soon they got to their feet, both of them laughing, and ran off together. They were headed home, he thought, also to surrender.

As he walked between the mud walls, one brilliantly yellow, one soft brown, he felt he was walking through time. He had often walked down this lane, but now he saw it as the street of his childhood. At the foot of the shaded wall, with treetops lifting over it, he and his childhood friend Varoosh used to toss coins, to see whose coin would land nearest the wall. He saw Varoosh, in a slight crouch, moving his arm back and forth as he aimed his toss, a silver glitter in the crook of his forefinger, turning his head now, in his comic way, to make some amusing remark to his friend about that skinny, guilty-looking man carrying a weighted umbrella through the sunshine.

Just here was a jube in which he and Varoosh used to sit listening to an old darvish they had befriended recounting his marvelous travels: his adventures among the Zoroastrians on the southern deserts, who feed the corpses of their dead to the birds; his springs and autumns as doctor to the Qashqai tribe during its migrations; nights in the opium gardens of Shiraz, where a poet would recite a ghazzal of Hafez and a nightingale would repeat it in the language of paradise; his days as magic-maker in the Isfahan bazaar; his year as camel driver with the great caravans of the deserts—the delights of the caravanserai, the magical taste of water hauled into the blazing daylight from quanats that ran many miles under the desert; his first glimpse of the ruins at Tahkte Jamshid, seat of the mightiest empire the world has known. . . . And at the urging of Varoosh, who was an Armenian Christian, the darvish also told of the strange, holy people in the Lebanon, which had been the western extreme of his travels.

Now Jamshid came to a doorway which had a bird of paradise for a knocker. Here he and Varoosh had sat and planned how they would run away and be darvishes themselves. He thought of how he had left his father's shop early one day and waited for Varoosh at the door of the Mission School. They had set out with a sheet of bread and a flask of curd-water. It was Varoosh's plan that they would go first to the Lebanon, where the miracle-hungry Christians would welcome these sunburnt, enigmatic travelers from the east. Varoosh told Jamshid about these people, their barbaric marvels—wanderings in the desert, burning bushes, roads opening through the sea, graves from which men arose as from a hotel bed, dying lepers suddenly feeling better, meals made of the Son of God's flesh, crucifixions in the sky. . . . Even Jamshid began to feel the bloodcurdling thrill.

He entered the street where the police station was located.

He remembered that night very clearly, though he had not thought of it for years. Where the desert begins, at the outskirts of the city, they had taken shelter in a half-ruined shrine dedicated to some rich wastrel claiming to have descended from the Prophet. When they broke the bread and poured the curd-water, Varoosh had assumed a tragical look and had said, "Take and eat. This is my flesh. This is my blood." Jamshid had been frightened and he was thankful it was not his god who was being mocked. He laughed and he ate. Each time he bit into the bread, Varoosh would wince.

The next morning Varoosh spread himself on the slope of the dome. He lay there slipping and hanging on, and obliged Jamshid to poke him in the side with a stick and to hand him up the flask of curd-water. He took a swig, couldn't hold on anymore, cried, "It is finished!" and leapt to the ground. Jamshid laughed too, but he was terrified.

Now he could see the red, white, and green flag slowly flapping over the door of the police station, as if trying to soothe the breeze that agitated it.

He remembered how cold they had been that morning. He had offered to go back and fetch sheepskin capes, but Varoosh, who had a deeper grasp of things, said it would be unnecessary, since they were returning home anyway to get themselves educated. A true darvish had to be educated, he told Jamshid, otherwise no amount of travels would do him any good.

Jamshid was not surprised when, a few weeks later, Varoosh's mother died in childbirth. Several days after the funeral Varoosh's family moved to Tehran, and Jamshid did not see Varoosh again. When Moharram came round a month later, Jamshid took part for the first time in the flagellation processions. He beat his head with a small flat sword, and made himself bloodier than anyone.

Jamshid stepped out of the sunlight, and into the darkness of the police station. Nobody was at the desk, so he sat down on the oaken bench. The door and windows were blazing with light. Another door led into a place of greater darkness. Jamshid cleared his throat loudly and coughed. Finally a policeman in a rumpled blue uniform came out. With hardly a glance at Jamshid he installed himself at the desk and began leafing through some papers. Jamshid went over and stood before him. Jamshid could feel the downward tug of the umbrella. The man continued to poke about in his papers. His face, Jamshid observed, was steeped in corruption. What was the good of giving himself up, he reflected, for doubtless the first thing they would do would be to try to make him bribe his way out again.

"I beg your pardon." Jamshid felt nervous and the words came out half strangled. "I have something to confess . . ." He stopped. The policeman had not deigned to raise his eyes. "I beg your pardon," he said, this time more loudly. The policeman glanced up, his pencil poised so as not to lose his place. Jamshid shifted uneasily. He realized suddenly it was no easy thing to confess to a murder.

"Ah, the rug-repairer," the policeman said, with a

tone of contempt, Jamshid felt. "What is it?" He lifted a haunch, grimaced, and farted. "We've got no rugs to repair, if that's what you're after."

"It's not that," Jamshid said. "It's that . . . it's that . . . I'm afraid . . . I . . ." He paused. How exactly to put it?

"Afraid, eh?" the policeman broke in. "Yes, it's a scary world. Holdups, murders, burglaries . . . Everybody's afraid. But," he showed his rotted teeth, "it's not to the police you must come when you're afraid. It's to the locksmith. When what you fear actually happens, then you come here. Not before." Agh! thought Jamshid, take a fool and put a wooly blue uniform on him and he believes he's the Shah himself, if he's talking to somebody of no importance. The man had turned back to his papers. Look at him, Jamshid told himself, pretending he can read!

"It's not that," he said, "not that at all." He was angry, and he was determined to confess no matter what, if only to force this goat to see how close he had come, in his insolence and stupidity, to letting a dangerous murderer slip through his fingers. But there are people for whom the world suspends itself, so as to give them the stage, and others whom it regularly interrupts and silences, and Jamshid was one of the latter kind. He had not failed to notice that if he was lecturing Leyla on her cooking, the doorbell would ring while he was in midsentence, or if he was complaining to a storekeeper, the man's telephone would cut him off with a rude jangle, or if he was haggling in the bazaar and just reaching, so he thought, an advantageous price, another person would jostle up and for half the price purchase the very item out from under his nose.

It was no surprise, then, that as he stood poised on the very brink of his confession, two men, cursing loudly and pushing each other, came banging into the station.

"This one whose father is a dog promised me three tomans . . ." one began. The policeman pushed his papers aside and gave the two men his complete attention.

"Your father fries somewhere," retorted the other. "I did not promise you one rial . . ." Jamshid went back to the bench and sat down. It would be some time if ever before that blue-suited oaf would be able to sort out the elements of the dispute. He felt light-headed. Looking through the window he could see the blue, wild shininess of the sky. Swallows were darting crazily through it. He saw the branch of a tree, out of which little leaves were starting to unfurl. He remembered how Varoosh used to criticize him for his timidity, his fear of authority. What would Varoosh be doing now? Had he really gone ahead and become a darvish? Probably. Probably he would have accomplished all the ambitions they had ever talked about. That was Varoosh's way. Jamshid experienced intense regret. Of all the adventures they had dreamed of, he, Jamshid, had not dared taste even one. He looked at the leaves again. How would it be, he thought, if one of them, even an unimportant one, should wither of its own free will and creep back into the limb?

He got to his feet, took up the umbrella, and walked to the doorway. On the threshold he paused and looked at the bright sunlight. He stuck his head out and looked down the street. It was empty, except for a little boy who stood in the sunshine looking back at him over his shoulder. In the room behind him the three men were still shouting at each other. Jamshid wavered a moment longer, then stepped out. For the first time in a long while, he was aware of how beautiful was the day.

Chapter Five

At a bakery Jamshid bought a sheet of sang-gak fresh-
ly plucked off the hot pebbles. Its warm, rough, fleshy
surface felt oddly pleasant. A few doors down he
bought a flask of curd-water, and stuffed both curd-
water and bread into his umbrella. At the corner he
glanced back toward the police station. Nobody
stirred. Ahead he glimpsed the same small boy still gazing back over his shoulder.

After cutting across some fields Jamshid came to the
road leading toward the southern desert, the same
road he and Varoosh had taken all those years ago. He
could see it stretching away, rising in the distance and
turning slightly under the great afternoon sky. The city
he was leaving was a low layer of greenery and white
buildings, out of which rose a few sets of minarets,
some blue, some mud-colored, and the golden dome of
the shrine. The sun made the dome glitter down one
side. There was no help now, Jamshid reflected. He
had plunged through. The world was closing up behind him. There was no possibility of turning back.
But the feel of the rutted, crumbling surface of the road
under his feet made him uneasy.

Had Akhbar returned to the shop bringing the police? Was that insolent dog at the desk even now suffering the wrath of his superiors? Or would that retribu-
tion have to wait until this evening, after Leyla had
begun to worry and had gone looking for him? It occurred to Jamshid that perhaps Leyla would lay out his

dinner, wait awhile, take it in again, eat her own dinner, sit in the garden for an hour or so, and then simply go to bed. He felt annoyed with her. In the morning she might not even notice his absence. The dead body might lie undiscovered indefinitely. He thought of the room where the sunpatch would be dividing, branching, starting to twist up the wall, and of the bloody body on the dark floor, growing muddier, merely a part of the shadows by now, a dark mass.

He did not feel tired as he walked, even though at precisely this hour, for some twenty years, he had not failed to lie down for his nap. Walking with long strides he felt the pull of muscles across his belly. The warm breaking surface of the road underfoot seemed more friendly now. The air cooled off and a breeze carried away his sweat. He concentrated on his step, and on the feel of gravel and pebbles through the cotton soles of his geevays. He thought of the old shirts and dresses these shoes were made of, worn by unknown men and women, thrown away, collected, torn into strips, the strips folded and hammered and sewn flat to flat, and worn again as these slightly spongy soles through which one could just feel the road's wrinkled surface.

He came to the ruined immanzadeh where he and Varoosh had spent the night. It was the same. Perhaps one or two more bricks had fallen off. That was the way. If things took a long time to get built, at least they didn't fall apart very fast, either. Lying against a heap of old tile fragments and broken bricks, Jamshid looked toward the horizon, pale where the sun had just lifted from it. He watched it vanish. Then he looked up and saw the sky was full of the beating lights of the stars. He looked around him and saw that the familiar things, stones, sands, rubble, had completely disappeared. He felt he was drifting alone out into the wilds of the night.

He reached into the umbrella for his bread and curd-water. As he did so his hand felt a sharp, stinging sensation, as if he had just been bitten or shocked. He drew the shears out and flung them into the darkness. They clanged on some rocks. He wiped his hand on his trousers, and took out the food. As he ate he seemed to smell the odor of blood.

He thought of Leyla, and all the cheerfulness went out of him. Surely she would be worrying. She was, after all, meek, helpless, and devoted. She would be pacing the garden in anguish. Before long she would go to the shop. . . . If ever he met anyone headed for Meshed, he would pay him a few rials to seek her out and say, "Your father wants you to know it was done because he loved you." Of course, the person would only pocket the money and forget the message. Just as well, for he had no idea why he *had* done it. In any event, Leyla's future, about which he had held so many hopes, lay smashed. That, at least, he was sure of. He raised his hand and examined it against the stars. It didn't look very real. Yet it had destroyed his own daughter. With the same hand he covered his face, and he began to sob. What good was it to have lived? He had lain forty years in the coffin of his narrow life. Suddenly he had stirred and it had cracked like an egg-shell. But too late. Only a dead thing lay within. It was as if he had thought all this time the purpose of being alive was to be able to say at any moment, "I am not dead." Perhaps he should turn back, as he and Va-roosh had done before. Perhaps he ought to get it all over with, rather than to protract it and live in misery. While he was thinking this he heard coming toward him the dull, empty banging of a camel bell.

Peering in the direction from which the sound came, he could only see the dim, gapped surface of the land. He had heard stories of roving brigands, descendants of the Assassins, who looted and murdered anyone who dared to travel by night in the empty southlands. Indifferently he waited what might come. The bell grew steadily louder. He could make out the shape of a camel lumbering toward him with slow, rubbery, des-ert tread. He could see the figure of a man leading it. It occurred to him this might be a policeman sent to fetch him. He hoped it was. It looked as if the camel was going to walk right over him, but a few meters away it stopped. The man walked over to him as if he divined him.

"Salaam alaikum." It was an old man's voice.

"Salaam alaikum," Jamshid said.

"It is cold, and we should have a fire," the old man said. With that he turned away. In a few minutes he came back with his arms full of twigs, desert grass, and a few sticks. Where there had been fires before, he kin-dled his fire.

In the firelight Jamshid saw an old, cunning, whim-sical face, very leathery and brown. "It will be slightly warmer tomorrow night," the old man said, "and slightly warmer the night after that. And so on. But for a few more nights we will need to have a fire." He went over to the camel and returned with a small threadbare carpet. He rolled himself up in it and soon fell asleep. After a while Jamshid lay down too, as close to the fire as he dared get. But because he was lying directly on the earth he could not sleep. He kept his eyes open lest at any moment it might seize him and drag him under.

Chapter Six

They would start walking before dawn, sometimes following the white dirt road, sometimes striking across the open land. Spring floods had cut gullies and the way was difficult. Sometimes the ground was so mushy with salt they sank in it. When the sun stood directly overhead they would stop in the shade of some rock, eat bread and water, and sleep. Ali, who had the carpet to lie on, would fall asleep at once. Jamshid, who lay on the earth, usually remained awake, more and more exhausted.

The old man showed no curiosity about who Jamshid was, and Jamshid asked no questions of the old man. He was only able to piece together that Ali had left his home years ago and now lived as a nomad trader, buying a camel load of what was cheap in one city and selling it in another where it was dear. He noted the saddle-bags were crammed with yellow and blue spoons from the plastic factory in Meshed. One morning Jamshid found the old man gazing about, muttering, "Where's Omar, Where's Shireen?" and cursing softly, and patting the camel affectionately, "Ah, poor Hassan!"

Jamshid asked Ali how he had managed to see him in the darkness that first night. "I didn't see you," Ali answered. "I heard you. From a long way off I heard you moaning to yourself. I am known as Ali of the Good Ears."

One night, while Jamshid was lying on his back

under the moon, trying to imagine an inviolable cloth under him that could protect him from the infections and insomnia-producing rays the earth gave off at night, Ali, whom he had thought asleep, addressed him quietly. "Do not move. A scorpion is walking across you. If he touches your skin you must not twitch or move a muscle."

No sooner had Ali spoken than Jamshid felt the creature touch the bare skin of his chest. He managed somehow not to jump but to keep his body rigid. He did not budge except to urinate in his trousers. The scorpion crawled forward, then sat still again. Would it never get off him? It crawled again. His scalp tingled. He was afraid the hair of his chest might stand on end and scare the scorpion into striking. Suddenly he realized he had lost track of where it was. He felt it here, he felt it there. Now a slow, stinging sensation took place on his neck, a sensation which was local and momentary, but which rippled out in all directions, breaking up his face, his chest, as if he were only an image. His life was over. What matter? He hated his life anyway, and the earth that killed you the moment you lay down on it. But he would take his killer into the grave with him. He reached for it, but he only felt his neck, perfectly unswollen. The moon was down, he saw, and the constellations had slid a long way. About his loins his trousers were damp and cold. He felt pleased with himself. A scorpion had walked across him, and he had merely pissed and dozed off.

The next morning Ali's comment was, "Is it a disease or is it just easier than pissing elsewhere?"

The land was rolling, heaved, and mountains were

always on the horizons. Sometimes the two men would see wild asses. They would get very close before the striped creatures saw them, bellowed, and went galloping off as if trying to be horses, but too top heavy. They would see gazelles in flocks that went wilting away, blown by a fast wind. Now and then Jamshid would see, perched on some outcropping of rock, a mountain goat in profile, standing up there still as a rock.

"By the way," Jamshid said one day. "Did you *hear* that scorpion that night?" When Ali shook his head his large ears shook. "No," he said, "By the moonlight I saw him crawling on you. The reason I knew the fellow was about was that he had just crossed over *me.*"

In the oasis city of Tabas they encamped in the Shah garden, under the shade of date palms. They remained several days, trading a few spoons for necessities. One afternoon, Jamshid was lying on his back in the grass, looking at the sky. He could hear a soft clicking noise, but he did not pay attention, for he was occupied with a thought. The thought was that they had put a carpet into this garden, that had been put in this oasis, that had grown in this desert, that lay in this world. He was unsure of the next step. Perhaps he should start at the beginning and try to go in the other direction. Now he noticed the odd noise again and looked toward Ali. The old man sat on the carpet, occupied with his feet. Jamshid cried out, threw himself forward, and snatched the trimming shears from the old man's hands.

"What are you doing with these?" he hissed, shaking all over. "Tell me what are you doing?" he shouted. The shears glinted in his hands.

"Cutting my toenails," Ali said, with only the suggestion of a smile. "But we must wash them," he went on. "There's a little bit of old blood on them." He reached out and took them back from Jamshid, and turned again to his toenails. He glanced up. "For it's a pity to throw away a good pair of shears."

Chapter Seven

For many days they moved south across the great desert. There were no mountains, grass, trees, streams, or even rocks. There was sand. Now and then they saw the ruts trucks had made the past winter, when the desert was hard enough to be driven on. Once they came to a mile-wide swath of ruts, where the sand had been soft and each truck had been forced to go wider than the last, to avoid sinking into the ruts of the trucks before it. Huge sand dunes had come rolling over these ruts in the meantime, and it looked as if the trucks had driven straight into the sand hills and disappeared.

The camel was walking more and more slowly, and the two men had to half drag it. Their bread had become light as paper. They softened it in their mouths for longer and longer periods, as they ran out of spittle. Ali had brought dates, which was what they mainly lived on. Jamshid could still not sleep. Worn out and half-starved, he felt he would not last much longer. He helped pull the camel not by strength but by the dead weight of his body wishing to fall forward. He also began to feel resentment toward Ali, who didn't mind anything, but kept on going like a machine. What a stupid old man, Jamshid would think, here we are, nearly dying, and he doesn't even notice it. Perhaps it was because the old man slept on the carpet that he did not tire. He began to hate him for it. One night it came to him that the only way to save himself was to murder

Ali and take the carpet for himself. Then, protected from the earth by the woven ornaments of paradise, he would rest as on a pure sunlit cloud.

The next morning Jamshid realized that he must be going out of his mind to have had such thoughts. He watched as Ali made tea. The man belonged to the things around him, and like them he was inaccessible. He poked the burning charcoal with his knobby hands and did not get burned. He seemed to live far away from himself. Aside from all points of right and wrong, Jamshid reflected, it would be impossible to kill this old man.

Later Jamshid made a point of inspecting the carpet. The knotted wool was nearly all gone and the carpet had only the airiest residuum of color and design left. It had once been a prayer rug, and the outline of the sacred niche, with its willow tree, was barely visible. In the old days Jamshid would have recommended this carpet be thrown on the trash heap. He persuaded himself as best he could that it was nothing to covet.

"Look in here," Ali said one morning. He pointed into the open mouth of the camel, who lay sleeping. "You see, he has only a few teeth left. It means he hasn't long to live. Camels use themselves up. I once knew an old man who died with all his teeth as if he expected there would be something to chew in the grave." A little while later Ali added, "I think if I were you I wouldn't worry about sleeping on the ground. There are worse fates than getting dirty."

The next day the green and white line of Yazd appeared on the horizon. Even Hassan the camel seemed to grow cheerful. At the Isfahan road, still some miles outside of Yazd, they found a coffee house. It looked very nice in its brilliant whitewash and its little blue Pepsi-Cola sign. Inside there were carpet-covered earthen platforms. On one of them sat two men puffing at waterpipes. Kicking off their geevays Ali and Jamshid squatted on the platform facing them.

The proprietor was happy to see the old man. "A long time since you've been by," he said.

"Years," Ali answered. "The trip is hard. I was glad I didn't have to make it alone. I only attempted it to see if I am too old. I think I am, for it has made me hungry as two lions. What do you have in the way of a chicken?"

"Many plump, tasty birds," the proprietor said, and beckoned them to the door of the courtyard. In the compound a dozen or so hens and one cock were pecking unhappily at the ground. "Let's feel that especially scrawny one there," Ali said, pointing to the fattest bird he could see, "and find out if there's any flesh on her at all."

"You mean this plump, tender thing?" the man said, and swooped a hen up by the neck. With much squeezing and poking the two men finally settled on a price. The proprietor unclasped a small rusty penknife and haggled at the head until it had nearly come off. It still dangled by a bit of skin when the proprietor flung the bird into the yard for bleeding. She set off at a fast run with blood pumping from her neck. Unbalanced by the dangling head, she ran in crazy directions. The cock appeared to think she was experiencing an unusual sexual frenzy for he went charging after her. When at last he caught up with her and leapt upon her she fell dead.

The proprietor shook his head. "A whore to the very end," he said sadly.

"Never mind," said Ali. "At least she died at work."

He and Jamshid went back into the coffee house to await their meal.

"She might have been ugly," Ali said, when they had gone back inside, "but she had a good figure. We will have a feast, for if the man doesn't know how to raise a chicken, he knows better than most how to cook one."

Jamshid noticed that the two men sitting there were observing them.

"You've walked down from Meshed?" said one, a thickset man with watery eyes. "Then you must have left town just about the time of the murder." Jamshid slupped tea from his saucer and stared at the ground.

"I don't know of any murder," Ali said.

"Then you're slow walkers," the thickset man said.

"Oh, it was quite a sensation," the proprietor put in. "Torbati, the famous mullah, was stabbed to death by a crazed carpet-repairer. The religious authorities have put up a reward of one thousand tomans for whoever brings him in dead or alive."

Jamshid at once felt resigned. He had never expected his escape to succeed anyway. But he resolved to give nothing away.

"Killed by a miserable rug-repairer whose daughter was a slut," the proprietor went on. "The good mullah had just been . . ."

"A slut?" Jamshid cried, cutting the man off in mid-sentence.

"Yes, indeed," said the proprietor, interpreting Jamshid's excited tone as a tribute to his narrative powers, "a very slut. A dog's son of a mason had laid her that very morning, it's said. The good mullah was just advising the poor fool her father to keep close watch . . ."

"Who says it?" Jamshid said, in a loud, quavering voice.

"Why, the radio says it," the proprietor answered, in an injured tone. "Who can you believe if you can't believe the radio, I'd like to know?" He retreated to his cooking.

The thickset man was whispering to his companion; presently the companion got up and went out. The man sat staring at Jamshid and making bubbles in his waterpipe. Ali and Jamshid ate their meal in silence.

Outside, Ali filled the waterbags and Jamshid hissed and kicked the camel to its feet. After they had moved on a way, Jamshid looked back at the coffee house. He saw the thickset man and the proprietor standing on a little rise with their shadows laid out before them.

The sun sank. The empty horizon bloomed a soft pink that quickly shrank to a thin green line. Behind them, over the place where Yazd would be, a full moon was coming up. They walked a long time without speaking, Ali leading the way across the sand. Near midnight, at a great rock, they sat down.

"Where are we going?" Jamshid asked.

"Shiraz," Ali said.

"I am sorry about the plastic spoons."

"Never mind. They will bring an even better price in Shiraz. In Shiraz they are crazy about plastic spoons. And I have a little house there, near the tomb of Hafez. My wife lives in it, waiting to give me a piece of her mind. She will take care of you until this thing blows over. Memories are short. Kill a policeman, and they hound you until you die. Kill a mullah and you've nothing to worry about. In his heart everybody dreams of killing himself a mullah. The reward is the nuisance. But in a little while the mullahs will see there are better uses for a thousand tomans than giving it away. I'll leave you in Shiraz, make the trip to Burijird, and by the time I'm back your crime will be forgotten."

It did not occur to Jamshid to protest or to express gratitude. And as he lay awake, he felt, for the first time since killing Mullah Torbati, the strange stirrings of possibility. Perhaps there was even a future. Even happiness. But why, he wondered, should this old man, who had a house and a wife, spend his days wandering around the desert, if happiness did exist?

"Why do you not stay in Shiraz?" Jamshid asked. But Ali snored comfortably. Those famous ears, Jamshid thought.

The moonlight shone in his eyes. He wondered what Ali meant by 'getting dirty'. It seemed to him, on the contrary, the whole point was to grow pure. After an hour or so he heard Ali whispering.

"They're coming, as I thought they might. They're following our tracks. They plan to kill us in our sleep." A smile came over the old man's wrinkled face. "But we will set the trap. Quick. Take Hassan ahead and make tracks so they will go on, thinking we had only stopped here to rest. I will wait in the shadows of this rock and give them a surprise." He hissed Hassan to his feet and handed the rope to Jamshid. "Now go," he said.

Facing him in the moonlight, Jamshid suddenly knew this savage old man was his friend. At bottom he understood it was of no importance whether or not he himself escaped. But he saw that Ali took it for granted that he would want to save himself. He did not like seeing this man put in danger for a trivial cause. Ali thrust the rope into his hands.

"But . . ." Jamshid began. Suddenly he felt fearful. But Ali was grasping the great shears in his right hand and his teeth glinted in the moonlight.

"Go," Ali said.

Chapter Eight

Walking fast, Jamshid made a wide turn and began to circle back. The moon gave him a qualmy sensation as he walked along. The camel's great head bobbed in the sky beside him. 'A slut,' the radio had said. He could see Leyla in his mind's eye, her eyes downcast, murmuring, "Yes, father, today I bought melons and cucumbers at the market as you instructed. Then I examined cloths in the bazaar for your new pajama. As the price was higher than you told me to pay I did not buy them. Then I came home, and first I swept, and then I cooked. . . ." An obedient girl, mild and respectful. Even if, from time to time, there seemed to be a hard shine in her eyes, impossible to be sure about, but suggesting hatred or contempt. Of course, if he looked a little carefully he could see her eye contained only the utmost meekness. 'Slut. . . .' Impossible. A pure, good girl. From infancy, completely pliable, completely amenable to her upbringing. He had cared for her twice over to make up for her not having a mother. Or thrice over, really, since she also got the affection that would have gone to his wife.

The moonlight drenched him as he walked across the sand. His mind blurred. Suddenly he remembered the time he had caught himself beating his daughter when she was small—or about to beat her—ferociously—for some trivial offense—or was it for none at all? And a year or so ago, when Leyla had malaria and he gave her a pomegranate, which he had kneaded to break up the cells within, and she had pierced the rind with her teeth, and sucked it, and all its juices had flowed out. Then she grasped his hand and drew him down on the bed beside her. Her lips were stained red and a trickle of pomegranate juice was running down her chin. She appeared in his eyes like some Ishtar of the old religions. "Kiss me, father," she said. He kissed her on the lips. With a shock he drew back. Was it only that he suddenly realized that she had become a woman, rich in passion like the woman he had lost, and had drawn back merely stung with desolation? Or in the mouth that pressed so yieldingly against his, did he think he could detect a buried sexual urgency? Or was it that he discovered a hideous element in his own feelings? Whatever it might have been, she had seen his fright only too plainly.

As he headed back toward the rock, he felt apprehension for Ali. Recalling that savage face he felt reassured. The night was silent and steeped in light. His thoughts went back to Leyla. 'A slut. . . .' He realized that on occasions when he had lost his temper with her it had been nearly always on account of boys. They had kept hanging around . . . Once he had broached the subject of marrying off his daughter to the wool-beater. "It's true, as a wool-beater, I beat second-hand wool," was all the man had said in reply.

Jamshid saw the great rock in the moonlight. As he approached it the world seemed to become deserted. A deadness came into the air. There was something poisonous about the moonlight. The rock alone seemed to live. A struggle seemed to be taking place on its glistening surface. Its black light cast straight down on the earth, illuminated a broken form. Jamshid ran over. In the blackness he found the body of the old man. The shears were sticking out of his chest just as they had out of Torbati's.

"Curse me to burn in hell," Ali whispered, bleeding at the mouth. "Five of them came . . . *five* . . . they saw me somehow . . . I got one on the arm . . . curse these ears . . . curse me for one who's getting old and deaf . . .," The blood was coming from his mouth. "They'll be back soon," Ali said. "Help me to the camel . . ." With his arms around Jamshid's neck he started to pull himself up. The blood that had overflowed from his mouth while he was on his back now poured down. He let go and fell back. He took hold of the shears and tried to pull them free. Unable to speak, he turned toward Jamshid with a furious, imploring eye. Jamshid took the old hands from the shears. Ali clutched at his hand; then the grip faded out.

"Take these remains back to Shiraz," Ali whispered, "I beg you, my friend."

Jamshid succeeded in getting the dead body lashed across the camel with the carpet covering it. Hassan rose with this burden into the moonlight.

Chapter Nine

Jamshid kept walking all night, through the yellow-green dawn, and into the daylight. He was moving automatically, only partly awake. It was not until nightfall that he reached rocky ground, where Hassan would not leave tracks. He lay down beside a spring, under some poplars that shut out the moon.

He awoke feeling the flopping of Hassan's jowls across his face. He sat up. It was the first glimmer of dawn. The camel's face, usually staid and sardonic, appeared now to be grinning. The half-closed eyes were almost satanic. There was blood on his face. Jamshid touched his own face. Blood came away on his hand.

Now he spied the bird that Hassan had just sliced in two. The black body lay a little way from the white head, with its peaceful, closed eyes. The head and body seemed parts of different animals. Jamshid got to his feet. A hole had been ripped in the carpet. Three other white-headed birds sat without moving in the farthest poplar tree. Jamshid took the rope and started forward again. When he looked back the birds were gone.

He leaned on the rope. The sun was hot. The corpse was starting to smell. He took the rope by its very end and walked faster, hoping to outpace the smell, but it seemed to lie in the air he was walking into. It was a putrid, sweetish odor. It was a flaw in nature, he thought, that a person should turn so abruptly into this smell.

In the afternoon, as he was passing some rocks, a man stepped out and came toward him. Jamshid wanted to ask the way. Apparently smelling the body, the man fell back.

"Wait," Jamshid said. "It's only my poor father I'm taking to burial. Don't be afraid, he had no disease."

But the man ran far among the rocks. Standing on a high rock so he could be seen, he called back, "Don't you know that if a man alone carries a corpse, the devil seizes him and stains him even to the ends of his nails, and he is unclean forever? Moslem dog! Be gone!"

Puzzled and shaken, Jamshid kept walking. He supposed it would be weeks before he could reach Shiraz. Even if he managed to keep off the birds, the flesh would have rotted. How was he to pass through villages while giving off this odor which no one could fail to recognize? It was a hopeless journey. If he was going to have to get rid of the corpse anyway, then the sooner the better. Maybe he should just chuck it where he was. Let the birds have it now, he thought, rather than later.

While he was wondering what he should do he came to a tower on a hillside overlooking the desert. He scrambled up the stone exterior to see if he could see any pursuers. As he came to the rim he paused and sniffed. Ali's very odor met him there. For it was a dokhmeh, a tower on which the Zoroastrians expose their dead to be eaten by vultures. Doubtless the man who had accused him by the rock was a Zoroastrian. On the circular roof were strewn a hundred or more human remains, most of them skeletons draped in bleached, torn clothing. A few were still bloody. They lay face up, the knees opened as if to first offer their genitals, source of most of their troubles. Jamshid wandered among them. He came to the bone-pit, a vast hole down the center of the tower, into which had been swept thousands of immaculate skulls and bones.

He had felt horror at first, but he grew accustomed to these open graves in about the time it takes eyes to grow accustomed to a change of light. This seemed the regular way to move, this picking his way through old, slightly stylized scraps of men and women—of children, too, he noted, stepping over some tiny bones.

He thought of what the old darvish had said about Zoroastrian customs. That to bury a dead man in the earth would befoul earth. That to drop him in the sea would befoul water. That to burn him would befoul fire. That to let him decompose would befoul air. It was for the birds, creatures who were essentially corrupt, and also, therefore, slightly sacred, to transmute dead flesh into the sky. Are the dead really foul? Jamshid wondered. It was true Ali was stinking. But it seemed to him now that if he had loved Ali it was not entirely for the shine of his spirit, it was also for the glittering darkness of his flesh and bones. Once the light was gone, was the remnant suddenly worthless and foul? Only his own nose, after all, was offended. God did not care about bad smells, nor did Hassan the camel. Nor did the sand and the sky. He decided, cost what it may, he would bear the corpse as far toward Shiraz as he could. In time, if he were faithful enough, his own nose might learn not to notice it. He went to the edge of the tower and put a leg over to descend. As he glanced down he failed to see Hassan.

Now he saw him, galloping across the desert in the sunlight, several birds hovering high above him. "Hassan! Hassan!" he called, but the huge panicked animal was in full gallop and out of earshot.

On the spot where the camel had been was a water flask and a dead bird. Jamshid picked up the flask and set out after the camel. Underfoot it was sandy again, and there were tracks to follow. He walked a long way. Night fell. It was one more night of bright moonlight.

At last he saw the hoof marks coming closer together. Soon he could make out Hassan's dark shape on the sand. A bird rose from it and vanished. The carpet had been torn. Much of Ali's flesh was gone. Jamshid bent by Hassan's head. With his fingers he drew up one of the great eyelids. The pupil inside wheeled itself down in the moonlight, and the eye was looking at the space occupied by Jamshid. He put his arms around the camel's neck and held its enormous, sorrowful face against his own.

Chapter Ten

When Jamshid opened his eyes he felt he could go no further, partly out of hunger and exhaustion, partly out of desolation. And partly out of a sense of cruel fatality. He had spent all those years in Meshed weaving closed the gaps, as if he had thought that if you perfected a surface what it was laid upon no longer had to be reckoned with. Now that he had broken through the surface, it seemed he had no choice anymore but to die into the essential foulness of things.

There remained the corpse of Ali to be carted to his native place. Only this called Jamshid out of his lassitude. He pulled himself onto the camel's back, just aft of the body. He hissed. Hassan opened his eye. Jamshid hissed and kicked. Hassan rumbled and slowly cranked himself into the air, hind and fore legs alternately straightening their hinges, until he stood upright. Jamshid kept himself just awake enough to steer the camel away from villages and to keep from falling off.

At intervals Hassan sank unbidden to the ground and dozed off. At these times Jamshid rolled off and rested beside him. The carpet-covered remains never left the camel's back. Nor was Jamshid any longer tempted to borrow the carpet to put between himself and the earth.

He could always sense the blackness of vultures in the sky. Never visible, they were a constant presence. One day it seemed to Jamshid the body was smelling less badly. Or was he now getting used to it? He smelled his own arm, and it seemed to give off the same odor. Through the shredded carpet Jamshid could see the corpse had become infested. It would be a miracle, he thought, if the corpse worms hadn't kept on going and infested Hassan too.

His perch went in lumbering circles, like the motion of a cow's jaws, or of soup being stirred. Sometimes as he rolled and pitched he actually smelt salt air, which came in little gusts and refreshed him. He imagined a boat on the sea must move this way too.

Now, as it seemed to Jamshid he was on his way to die, he began to think of his dead wife. It had always been painful for him to think of her. Whenever he had visited her grave with its one red brick for a headstone, he had restricted himself to the forms of propitiating the dead. As for memories of her while she lived, he did not like them or want to probe into them.

It was a mistake to begin with, that marriage, Jamshid thought. He had been but twenty-two and Cobra only fourteen. His father had arranged it in the last months of his life, so as to leave no loose thread behind. It brought to a close a decade of piety and hard work, begun the day Varoosh had left Meshed, while just a boy. Though she was young, she had been strong and graceful, with huge black eyes and a straight, rich, sensual mouth. He had fallen in love with her at once. He had been immediately aware, too, that this love was not returned. He had sensed catastrophe, but he had reasoned that marriage itself might well even the balance, giving some love to her side, and if necessary taking some away from his own.

The ground began to rise. Hassan had to go more slowly. Jamshid thought back on the early days spent repairing the torn carpets and trying not to think too much about Cobra. After the evening prayer he would come home and sit by the pool in the garden, smoking the waterpipe, watching Cobra preparing the evening meal. He was moved by her grace, and increasingly disturbed by her aloofness and mystery. Sometimes she seemed direct and open, and often she was in good spirits. But just as often she would start brooding for reasons Jamshid never discovered. So it would go. She would listen attentively when he talked and if he tried to make a joke she would laugh. Before long she seemed only to be trying to focus on his words and stopped bothering to laugh. Far from understanding what she was feeling at these times, he did not even know what he felt himself. The only thing he knew was that she had become an obsession. He had been brought up to think that a wife was a minor adjunct in one's life, and he was bewildered at the turn this marriage had taken. When at last he did decide to assume the traditional male role and subdue his wife through force of tradition, it was as a last resort.

He told Cobra how to dress and carry the chaddor; how to shop; how to serve foods; how to divide up her day; how to show and not show her feelings; and so on. Thus he hoped to gain mastery and turn her into a true wife. It had begun well enough. And for a little while after Leyla's birth Jamshid actually believed he might win her complete submission, which he was ready to accept as the next best thing to her love. But soon he observed a distinct slackening. He redoubled his law-giving, only to find worse instances of her falling off. One day he told her she was to keep her face from the sunlight so that the skin might remain pale. Not a week later he came home to find she had been playing with the baby for hours with her face and neck exposed and was brown as the earth. He made it clear he did not want her mouth or one hair of her head to show in public. The next day he looked from his shop window to see her crossing the street with her entire head uncovered to all viewers. After each transgression he would lecture her, at first patiently, and at last angrily, in a style he had picked up from his father. Nothing helped. All his efforts turned out to be self-defeating. The more he demanded, the less he got. The gulf between them had been very wide, when, eighteen months after their marriage, while Jamshid was engaged in prayer at the Shah Mosque, Cobra died.

Jamshid had been on the point, he often told himself, of trying to reach across to her. But now he understood he had been afraid to try. It occurred to him that perhaps Cobra's death had come to him almost as a relief. It had been Mullah Torbati, he reflected bitterly, who had helped him shut her from his mind by intimating that from the fact that she died it could be deduced that she deserved to die.

They were mounting a steep rock slope, and Hassan was laboring unnaturally. His life back in Meshed appeared by comparison unreal, made up as it was of rules that only spoiled any chances there might have been. The words 'slut' and 'murderer' lost their meaning. All that seemed important now was to bring the remains of Ali back to the earth of Shiraz.

Hassan gained the top of the rock hill. As he began to descend, he lost his footing and fell heavily on his side. Jamshid was thrown to the ground. He got up and urged the camel to right itself. It heaved into a crouch, but at once toppled over again. Bending beside him Jamshid lifted an eyelid. It came up with difficulty. The black pupil remained wide open, looking into the absolute darkness. When Jamshid let go the eyelid dropped halfway down, giving the camel a comical, drowsy air.

A few feet away, in the stone cliffside, Jamshid saw the entrance to a cave. He separated the two corpses, and dragged Ali's toward it. Inside it was cold and very dark. He went out to the saddle bags and got a candle. By its light he found an open, scooped out sarcophagus, made of the stone that is called 'flesh-eating'. It seemed to be waiting for a corpse. He put Ali's corpse into it arranged more or less in the order of life. Then he stretched himself out on the stone floor. It took great effort to rise on an elbow. As he drew in his breath to blow out the candle he noticed the point of the flame, that shifting instant where the flame was turning into pure spirit. Then he blew it out. His bones seeming to lie directly against the stone, he fell into deep sleep.

Chapter Eleven

When Jamshid woke it seemed more pleasant in the cave than when he had fallen asleep. During the night he had come to terms, it seemed, with the stone and darkness, and the corpse smell had vanished. He went toward the light.

The framed sunlit scene seemed set up for him as an ultimate landscape of desolation. Before him was a vast field of stone ruins—ruins that were pure and absolute, that gave little hint of what they had once been except that whatever it was had been of an extraordinary magnificence. Below him hundreds of empty pedestals stood carefully spaced out on the ground. Around them on four sides were the frameworks of vanished walls, walls of nothing in which the empty frameworks of doors and windows opened their holes. Beyond, on a distant rise, were many huge fluted columns, some broken, some reaching the old altitude, holding up nothing. Jamshid realized this place was Takhte Jamshid, the Throne of Jamshid, the ruins of what had once been the springtime capital of Iran in its greatness. The cave in which he stood was a tomb to house the remains of one of the Achemenian kings. Brushing the old dust from his pajamas, Jamshid stepped into the sunlight.

It was the afternoon light.

Nearby he saw Hassan's bloody skeleton. While Jamshid had slept, the camel had been almost entirely devoured. The harness still wrapped the empty, scraped bones, the saddle frame still gripped the lost back. The saddlebags had been torn off and ripped open. Blue and yellow plastic spoons lay scattered about.

He saw the face of Hassan as he had last seen it, drowsy, even dead keeping an ineradicable haughtiness. He thought of burying what was left, but the hill was rock, with only tiny pools of sand. If it was the nature of birds to eat this flesh, let them eat it. If it was the nature of the sun to bleach bones, then let it bleach these.

To cover the remains of Ali, Jamshid walked back and forth many times between the sunlight and the cave, carrying handfuls of sand. When he thought he had put on enough sand to cover the body he lit the candle. He was surprised to see the handles of the shears still sticking out of the body. For a moment he was back in his shop in Meshed, bending over the dead mullah. The saddle had pressed the shears deep into the breastbone. When he thought they were coming free, he saw it was only that the whole rib cage was beginning to lift off. He tried to push it down again but sand had slid under, and he had to bring in more sand. He left the shears where they were. As the candle gutted and gave a last flare, he pressed his hand into the sand, leaving a hand print, the mark which peasants, with painted hands, put on the walls in their villages, in remembrance of the martyrs.

Jamshid rolled up the torn carpet, made a sling for it of straps from Hassan's harness, and hoisted it on his shoulder. He paused a moment. He looked up into the sky. Nothing was visible in the glittering air. He knew that in that blueness lived the changed flesh and blood of Hassan. Those strange, bobbing, rubbery motions of the camel had been, all the time, a way of trying to become winged.

Jamshid stumbled down the rock hillside and entered the field of ruins. A huge stone animal, half lion, half dragon, looked over the plains. Jamshid circled it and saw that its body had fallen off and lay slain on the sand. He climbed a staircase; beside him ascended a panel of climbing men carved in relief, each wearing a different costume, each bearing a different gift, a panel depicting the entire known world coming here to render homage. At the top, where these emissaries should have laid down their gifts and knelt in fealty, was nothing now but the emptiness. Jamshid saw a great stone slab set up high in the air bearing a scene in relief: under the protection of a man carrying an umbrella and another carrying a fly swatter, the king was on his morning walk. Where his head should have been was only broken stone. Jamshid kicked at a stone or two on the ground to see if he could turn up the face. He passed through a doorway; he could as easily have passed through the wall. He reached the highest elevation of the ruined field. On stone slabs he saw writing in the square script of the foreigners. He wondered what urgent messages they had chosen to record.

Dusk fell. Jamshid decided to sleep where he was. He did not spread out the carpet. It didn't matter to him that he lay directly on the earth. But as he lay there he felt the strangeness of this material under his hands—an earth made of stones that had been grated, rained, blown, and burnt into a substance that was hardly earth at all, but a form of disappearance, a substance into which one of the world's great empires had gone away. As if death had been ground up and strewn here in a thick layer. He saw the jagged, unburdened columns rising in the darkness and the great stones with their heavy, closed eyes.

He lay a long time hearing the noise before he started listening to it. It was an eerie, anguished crying, half a scream, half a wail, as if some being in the ruins were keening for all things. It was the most anguished sound he had ever heard. As he lay listening he thought he heard in it also a kind of ecstasy.

The sound grew nearer. Though the moon had not yet risen, he now could make out in the darkness a human figure moving among the stones and columns. The wail broke out again. It occurred to him that whoever it was staggering through the night was grieving for one particular lost thing. For anything at all, perhaps, as long as it was *one* thing.

"What is it, woman?" Jamshid said. "Why do you wail?"

Continuing to stagger toward him the figure cried in response, "My son! My son! I have lost my son!" She came closer. "If you are a Moslem you will help me!" Jamshid could see her face. Her eyes were shining with tears, her mouth was large with crying.

"Tell me," he said, coming up beside her and putting a hand on her arm, "what has happened to your son?"

She turned and looked at him and kept on wailing. Was it the bad light, here in the darkness, Jamshid thought, that produced the look of sexual passion in her face? But he heard it in the wail itself. She put her arms around Jamshid. Strangers, they stood clinging to each other under the faceless king. Her own face shone ivory in the starlight, her eyes glittered. Continuing to hold each other, they sank to the ground.

"What happened to your son?" Jamshid asked, as much to distract himself from his need for her as to find out.

She only kept wailing, "My son! My son!", though more calmly now. At last the wails passed into whispers; at last the whispers turned into deep-taken breaths, and the woman fell asleep in Jamshid's arms. Jamshid himself slept little, dreaming intense sexual longings, experiencing them again whenever he woke.

The earth on which they lay was glistening, though the moon had not yet risen. He took some in his hand and let it run through his fingers. It shone and sparkled, and seemed to have something in it of the iridescence of certain feathers.

In the morning she was gone. There were great wings of light in the east. From far off he heard a rustle and splashing, and a hollow, fluting music. He got up and followed the sound. At the edge of the ruins he came to a wide, shallow well. When he lowered his bucket many doves, which had been bathing, burst into the air. He drank in long gulps. He took off his clothes and poured cold water all over him.

He came to a little mud house where some peasants were sitting in the shade and inquired of the road to Shiraz.

"That is the very road."

As Jamshid walked down the Shiraz road, he heard a car approaching. He stopped and faced it and signaled that he wanted a ride. It was big and shiny and two foreigners sat in the back seat. One pointed at him and they seemed to be laughing. For a long time Jamshid could see the car's dust proceeding across the Mardasht plains, and hear its motor.

Later in the day a melon truck came along. Jamshid hailed it and it stopped. Beside the driver sat the driver's wife and children. "Get in the back," the driver said. "You may sit on the melons but take care you don't step on them."

Jamshid climbed on top of the truckload of green and white striped melons, and the truck set off. He felt around for a ripe one and broke it in pieces on the railing of the truck. In dripping handfuls he devoured it as he rode into the wind and across plains that were, suddenly, green and fertile.

Chapter Twelve

In Shiraz Jamshid washed the melon juice from his hands at a public tap, and made his way to the tomb of Hafez, near which he hoped to find Ali's house. All he could do was tell Ali's widow of the old man's death, and the whereabouts of his remains.

As for Hafez' remains, these lay in a garden of quiet green pools, and ancient cypresses and dogwood trees. In the center of the garden, under a little canopy set on eight columns, was the coffin. It was made of stone and on its sides verses were cut. Jamshid wondered what they might say and wished now that he had learned to read. Everywhere were flowers and their reflections. No wonder, thought Jamshid, Ali had wanted to be buried in Shiraz. Here death seemed to be unblurred by darkness or pain. After ordinary life, it was like a step forward.

As he stood at the coffin Jamshid noticed a yellow-faced old man beside him. Touching the coffin with one hand, the man seemed to be praying. Tears splashed from his closed eyes. From his pocket he drew out a volume of Hafez' poems, opened it, and put down his finger. Jamshid saw the yellow face expand in a smile.

"Listen," the man said, turning to Jamshid, "hear what Hafez has said to me: 'Time stops not, take the Rose of Love in your arms.' How is that for advice? Ah, Hafez. . . . It seems that he knows us, each of us, so well . . ."

"But, old man," said Jamshid, for the man appeared to be close to a hundred, "what on earth can you do with advice like this, which is more fit for a boy of twenty?"

Jamshid had only meant to be sensible but he saw he had offended the yellow-faced man. "What do you know of a man?" the fellow said. "At half my age you are already wizened. Look how pathetic and skinny you are." He rattled Jamshid's shoulder. "You think you can tell me what a man can do or cannot do. You look to me as if you've never seen the Rose of Love at all . . ."

Jamshid was only too aware that, as far as he was concerned, the Rose of Love had never so much as blossomed but only budded and died. He started to defend himself. "Why just last night, by the dark of the moon . . ." But his long life mostly without love came back to him, and he tasted ashes. He was wizened and disgusting. So he would be until death, so he had been since birth. Or at least since he had turned back from that adventure outward with Varoosh. And there was no point in saying 'until death': in all important respects he had already died. "Never mind, old man," Jamshid said, "I am sorry for what I said."

"Now," the old man went on, placated at once, "let us see what the poet has to say to you." He held out the book. "Just open the book where it opens, and put down your finger where it puts itself down." The old man studied the line on which Jamshid's finger had touched down. "For you," he said, "the augury is this: 'Who is it comes dancing on the grave?' He studied the phrase and nodded his head. "A deep saying," was all the exegesis he offered.

Poets of mystical inclination irritated Jamshid, because they gave the impression of high significance and yet kept hidden exactly what it was. This incomprehensible question irritated him now. Why did he have to get a question anyway, instead of straightforward advice? The old man, who would have been content with any utterance, the cloudier the better, was given an unequivocal prescription that a fool could see was preposterous. That, Jamshid reflected, is the way with poetry. When it is incomprehensible it strikes you as profound, and when you do understand it, it lacks common sense.

The flush of poetic pleasure still showed in the old man's eyes. It embarrassed Jamshid, and he decided he had better go about his business of locating Ali's widow. He asked the old man if he knew the neighborhood.

"I do," the man said. "I live nearby and stroll over here every evening to get my augury. I have done so for as long as I can remember. By now I have received nearly every one in the book. Every night it comes true. But yours . . . I have never known anyone to have received that one. A very deep saying . . ."

The old man sensed Jamshid's impatience and got back to the point. "I live over there. Where that palm grows up out of a garden. Will you come and eat with me? I am a poor old man and have not much to offer. But I think you are poorer still and will not object."

Jamshid protested only a little, for it did seem to him this was the wrong time to call on Ali's widow. To show up just at dinner time was certainly impolite. Furthermore the poor woman might have no heart for cooking, on hearing the news. And Jamshid had never been hungrier. Protesting a few times more, according to custom, he went along.

In the twilight, under the date palm, they ate melons, pomegranates, rice, mutton, eggplants, and curd-water. Then they smoked the waterpipe. It made a loud purring noise in the garden. Finally the old man got to his feet.

"Now for our auguries to come true. Wait," he said, "I will be back directly."

Chapter Thirteen

The old man came out of the house carrying an opium pipe. When the pipe had heated up in the fire, he cut a morsel of opium, yellow-brown as his face, and pressed it to the bowl. Holding a red-hot piece of charcoal to it, he blew down the pipe until the coal turned white hot in the jet of air and started the opium burning. It crackled and hissed as he sucked its smoke deep into his lungs.

He handed the pipe to Jamshid. "To help you find the meaning of your augury."

"Do you feel anything?" the old man asked. Jamshid only tasted burnt smoke, the almost cloying richness of something dank and moldy that suddenly dries out by burning. Jamshid thought of the poppies, their waxen blooms in the fields, made for the eye. He could see their sap flowing by night from their wounds, to be breathed into a man's blood, in some garden of flowing water and roses.

"I am feeling the blessing of opium," the old man said, preparing himself a fourth pipe. "All day I miss the blessing. All day I am dead for lack of it. But every evening I come back to life. The blessing is the relief of no longer being dead. If only I could be dead and not know it. I used to wish I never took up smoking. Now I am very old, and to wish would be unseemly. Look at how these hands jump and tremble. Never mind . . ." He sighed and handed the pipe to Jamshid. "My only regret now is the price you've got to pay for decent opium . . ."

"Never mind," he repeated, "I am alive again. That is all that matters. Smoke your pipe. An old man, who has been dead many times, tells you this. To be alive is all that matters."

Jamshid sucked in the smoke, holding it a long time in his lungs, not letting one wisp escape until he had got the best of it.

"Do you know why I brought you to my house to-night?" the old man continued. Jamshid shook his head. "Because when I saw you standing at the tomb I knew you were a dead man."

"Will opium bring me back to life?"

"No, I don't think it will," the old man said. "It brings me alive, it's true, but that is because it is what I died of. I don't know what you died of. Whatever it was, that is what will bring you alive again. However, smoking will tell you what it is to live. It will show you a picture of yourself fully alive. What do you feel now?"

Jamshid put down the pipe. He was a little abashed to answer.

"I think of my wife," he said.

"Ah!" the old man replied, "It is like that the first few times. But later . . . And is she a good woman?"

"A good woman? . . ." Jamshid muttered. Suddenly he saw his wife's black eyes with little lights in them in the darkness, the night of their wedding. It was like remembering what he had never perceived—a look containing some shuddering, animal mystery.

"She was young. To me, she was beautiful," he said. "She was obedient, and also disobedient. She was graceful and her eyes were black. I mourned for her but perhaps I never truly missed her until just now."

"She is dead?"

"She is long dead."

"Marry again," the old man said. "I can guess now at the sense of your augury. You died on account of love, and love has to bring you back again. You must dance on your grave."

Jamshid smiled. He felt an affection for the old opium smoker. He was discovering there were possibilities of friendship in the world. For the first time he found himself wanting not to be caught. "To live is all that matters." He thought that it might be true.

"There is someone I must find," he said. "An old woman who lives hereabouts. Maybe you know her. She is the wife—the widow—of an old man named Ali—Ali of the Good Ears—a great man who has been gone from Shiraz many years, traveling about with camels . . ."

"Ah, Ali the murderer," the old man said. "Yes, I knew him well. I am truly sorry he is dead. His wife lives just two houses away. I will go and tell her you are here. In the last few weeks she had said more than once she expected to have news of him. I am sorry for her that it will be bad news, but to tell the truth she has been living with the ghost of that old man for too long. Tell me how he died." The old man smoked a fresh pipe as he listened to the story.

"His death was like him," he said when Jamshid had finished. "He was the noblest murderer of his day. He used to be a looti in the days before there were policemen. He kept it up even after the policemen came, because none of us around here could really trust a policeman to protect us.

"Ali was everything a looti should be. He was brave,

manly and patient and kept his promises. He was pure and single-minded. He didn't oppress the weak or commit extortion against anyone. He drove evil away from anybody who was oppressed. He spoke the truth, and listened to it. He gave out justice even against himself, and never hurt anybody whose salt he had eaten. Hypocrisy to him was shameful, and he didn't worry about calamity.

"Well, one winter everyone in the quarter was getting sick, and a little boy died. At last it was discovered the baker had been putting poisoned corn in his bread in order to save money. Ali went to the baker's shop and was about to throw the baker into the oven, according to custom. The baker was screaming and wriggling, for Ali had the wretch poised at the fiery door. Just then a policeman rushed in and struck Ali across the cheek with a club. Ali understood a new order was coming, and if the policeman hadn't struck him, I believe he would have let him rescue the baker. But having been struck, Ali dropped the baker and struck the policeman on the head. The policeman died on the spot. I found him just standing there. He would have waited until the rest of the police had got up their nerve and come for him. But I told him he must go. His wife, who was only a little girl then, said she would wait for him as long as it might be. Once in a while, every few years or so, he came back, but it was no good. He was too famous. One dead policeman never blows over. Wait here," the old man said, getting up, "I will go and tell Ali's wife that his friend has come bringing news."

Left alone, Jamshid began to feel strange from the

opium. Any scene his senses fixed on became immobile. "Who is it comes dancing on the grave?" He sat in the lamplit garden gazing at a rose which, head bent against the wall, clasped itself. Inside the rose a fly lay motionless in sleep. The lamp put shadows on the mud wall. The wall was not a surface but a depth across which moved living, glorious forms. Jamshid smelled the sharp, desolating smell of dried mud. A palm tree rose up horny as a snake. At the top huge orange sprays of dates lunged downward again, and dark, sword-like leaves clashed slowly in the sky. The dark odor of the dates floated down. The pool of water shifted a little and then heaved.

"She is still awake," the old man said, coming back into the garden. Jamshid heard the voice very dimly. He had to shake his head to free himself. "She asks that you go to her. At this very minute she is preparing tea for you. Go. Her house is two doors away."

Jamshid took up his carpet. As he closed the gate behind him it was like closing a door on a world of signs, the sign the book had given him and those woven into the garden itself all telling him to go.

Chapter Fourteen

The world of the widow's garden had its signs too. When the widow turned and passed Jamshid tea he glimpsed her eye and a bit of her face. He had assumed she would be near Ali's age. He saw she was much closer to the age his own wife would have been. Her eyes were black, and lights seemed to float in them. He dropped sugar into his tea and drank from his saucer. She took and refilled his glass. When he had finished she came over and touched the rolled-up carpet.

"He is dead then?" she asked. These were her first words. They were in the lovely Shirazi accent.

"Yes," Jamshid said.

"Did he die of disease, or was he killed?" she asked without a sign of emotion.

"Killed."

She nodded. "And you were his friend?"

Jamshid paused. In a way he had become Ali's friend after the man was dead. He nodded.

She was kneeling close to him. She hesitated, and then she said, "And you—are you a murderer too?" Jamshid wanted to deny it, or to put it in a less harsh way, but she had already seen his acknowledgment. She rose and went into the house. Jamshid felt it was time to leave. He had done what had to be done.

As he got up to go she reappeared. She was carrying bedclothes in her arms. She spread them on a wooden trestle by the pool. "You may sleep here," she said. "It is late, and you have traveled far." She herself went to the other side of the pool and got into the other bed.

As Jamshid lay in the darkness the effects of the opium made him feel innocent, childlike. He saw the stars. He remembered long ago, his wife beside him, looking up and seeing them framed in the nearly perfect rectangle of his garden in Meshed. He remembered how he had gone over the sky night after night, until it had become for him like a vast carpet, until he did not see its bizarre dippers, hunters, or lyres but the familiar dolmehs, fylfots, trees, and holy birds that lived in carpets. Now he saw them only as wild stars. They seemed terribly near, as if soon he would be lying among them. They grew larger and larger. It seemed they were rushing downward toward him, mouths of light opening and shutting. He could hear their bright yapping. He could smell their breaths, the scent of burnt stone. Then their downward rush stopped. It seemed they were moving outward again. Something near at hand caught his attention.

Across the pool he could see the bed where the widow lay in the darkness. Lights floated in the water between them. And where the widow lay it seemed he could make out other, fainter lights, as though she lay open-eyed, her eyes, too, full of reflections. But he heard her steady breathing, that had in it some rhythm like that of the stars. He said nothing.

When he awoke it was bright daylight. At dawn, as he lay looking up, he thought, marvelous, that a man can dream fearful things in the darkness and awaken suddenly to see carefree swallows flying in the bright sky.

He thought of the widow. He felt shame. He who had felt lust for no woman but his wife—and in a dream the mad woman of the ruins—had fallen asleep lusting after the mourning widow of his friend. Closing his eyes again, he lay there reproaching himself. So this is what comes of committing one sin; before long you start committing them all.

He resolved he would return to Islam and become as devout as once he had been. The first step, obviously, was to get up and say the morning prayer. He had not prayed once, he realized, since the morning of the murder.

He got up. He would pray, and after morning tea, head for the police station. At the pool he splashed stagnant water on his feet, arms and face. It smelled badly and left him smeared with slime. He unrolled what remained of Ali's carpet. The ground showed through in a dozen places. It was dark with old blood. It made him think of Ali. For Ali had been just such a person, bloodstained, worn, and ripped, in whom the earth gleamed.

He pronounced a takbir to cut himself off from worldly things for the duration of the prayer. He took his stand facing the quibla. But as he raised his arms he saw the widow. She was watching over a little pink-ribbed teapot which sat in the coals. There was energy and grace in the way she squatted. She reached toward the teapot with a motion slow and definite. As she did so her chaddor pulled tight at her flanks. She took up the teapot gingerly and held it very close o her. To pour she tilted her body to one side, to stop pouring she straightened up again.

"I've got to clear my head," Jamshid thought, and he went over to her. Without raising her eyes she handed him the glass. Then she drew a slab of new bread from the little oven in the corner of the garden. She offered him bread with honey. He squatted down beside her and looked at her but she kept her eyes averted.

"Did you sleep well?" she asked. The eyes of a woman who wears a chaddor get to be as expressive as an entire face, but these eyes said nothing. Jamshid wondered if he even existed for her.

"Like the dead," he said, regretting his metaphor. "Except I had a dream."

"A good dream?"

"A hideous one. And late in the night, too." Dreams that come late in the night were the ones that come true. Jamshid did not go in for dream-reading, but he saw the widow did.

"You must tell me your dream," she said, suddenly animated. "If you don't, your hair and beard will curl right up."

"Well," said Jamshid, "in the first dream I was working in my old shop — I used to be a rug-repairer — and I was looking at the sunlight on the floor beside me. I was knotting in the head of a bird — a white bird I think — when a shadow came across the embroidered curtain on the window. I got up and tore the curtain away. Instead of a window I found a dim room. In it sat a man covered from head to foot with wounds and running sores — he looked at me and said, 'Jamshid! Jamshid!' . . . there was more . . . I have forgotten it." Jamshid turned to her. The widow was gazing gravely at him.

"It is a 'woman's dream', let's hope," she said in her quiet voice. "One which means something deeper than what it says. Let's hope it means that inside you will be well even if outside you are sick and hurt." She spoke these words so that Jamshid understood she felt concern for him. Until then she had seemed to live and move only by necessary impulses.

As Jamshid drank his third glass of tea he remembered the police. Yet the sky had never been so blue and seldom had he felt so happy. Perhaps he would sit just awhile longer before turning himself in. He might as well get well rested up, in case the police should want to question him at great length.

"Do you mind if I sit around awhile?" he said.

"Sit," the woman said. "You were Ali's friend and now you are my friend too."

He watched the widow as she went about her chores. He fell into daydreams of starting a new life. If only the police don't hang me, he thought. Let them do anything, but not hang me. He wondered what a new life would be like. It could not be anything like the old one, he knew that.

A knock came at the door. Jamshid saw the widow put her eye to the peephole, then come quickly toward him. He already knew what she had seen.

She seized his hand, closed her eyes a moment, then said, "Come!"

She took him into a dark room. "Wait, I will be back soon." As she went out she accidentally brushed against him.

Chapter Fifteen

"Murdered as he merited, if I may say so," an official-sounding voice was saying. "And with that dog's son of a carpet-repairer's big carpet shears sticking right out of his chest . . ."

"Quarreling," another voice was saying, "unless I'm much mistaken. The one was as evil-tempered as the other . . ."

In the darkness Jamshid felt shock and anger. Would the widow believe that he himself had killed Ali?

"A murderer the like of whom hasn't been seen in this country for a generation . . ."

"Bloodthirsty as a lion. Cunning as a Zoroastrian. Strong as a strength-house champion. He had to be, to manage to kill, begging your pardon, that vicious old man . . ."

The voices moved out of earshot. Nearly in tears of frustration and anger, Jamshid lay back on the bed to await the widow's return. Would she betray him? But the minutes passed, and the police did not burst in. Or was she reserving the delights of revenge for herself? They would pay the thousand tomans for him dead just as well as for him alive.

There was a sudden moment of light in the room, as the door opened and closed.

"Widow," Jamshid said, "is that you?"

"It is," came back her expressionless voice.

"Widow," he said, "I beg you, get a candle, I hate the darkness."

71

After a few minutes she returned with a sputtering candle. She came over to him holding it in both hands. As the flame wavered it made a dark flashing across her face.

"Listen," Jamshid said, sitting up. "They lie. Ali was killed by five dog's sons of Yazdis. I . . ." He stopped short. A look of anger had crossed the widow's face.

She put down the candle and took Jamshid's hand. "I am angry with you for thinking I would believe the police," she said. The chaddor had slipped off; her entire face and her hair were visible. The flame of the candle swayed again and black shadows moved in her features. She smiled at him. His head was clear. He saw her in a reality beyond the reach of opium. On the little bed, in the light of the candle, they made love.

When they came into the garden, it was evening. They sat by the pool and ate a meal of rice, fruit, and Shirazi wine.

"So long as they think you killed Ali," she told him, "they will not look for you here. You will be safe. I wish you to stay, if you would like."

"I would like to," said Jamshid. He began to foresee what a new life might be like. It even seemed possible he could assume another name, learn another trade, grow fat and unrecognizable. He could mail money to his daughter, perhaps one day send for her . . .

The night was warm, one of the last of the true summer nights. There were many stars. In bed they lay close together and they kissed. As he slid his body on top of hers he was aware, for a moment, of the dark ragged trees all around them. He gave a laugh. Then he knew nothing but their bodies, their mounting, hardly bearable rhythm, her moans which broke into a wild, happy cry as they shuddered into each other.

In the morning the air was still warm. The stars were still crawling across the darkness. He drew the covers back and looked at the widow's body. He thought he had never seen a person so beautiful. He put his arm across her belly. She remained asleep, making purring, pacifying noises that were not quite snores.

Someone was shaking him awake. He opened his eyes to see the widow and the yellow-faced opium smoker crouched beside him.

"Tell him," said the widow.

"They know you didn't kill Ali," the old man said. "On learning who it was they killed, the Yazdi dogs have stepped forward and claim a reward. The police captain is sitting in my garden, having a pipe before he comes here. You must leave at once."

When Jamshid had dressed, the widow put bread and cheese in his pocket. She rolled up the carpet, put it in its harness, and hoisted it to his shoulder.

"It's yours," Jamshid protested. "I was bringing it back to you."

"I give it to you," the widow said.

"As soon as I can I'll come back," Jamshid said.

"Yes."

Chapter Sixteen

The first person Jamshid saw in the street was a policeman. He turned and walked in the other direction. He saw some men asleep on the sidewalk, apparently workers from a construction. He spread his carpet beside them and lay down. Where his hand fell it touched the earth. He could see the little room again, with the light from the candle swaying ever so slightly on the wall. "Are you contented?" she had asked him. "I know you are, I am too." The impassive quality of her voice now appeared to him as the deepest tenderness. "I loved Ali when he was my husband, but when many years go by and a man remains absent, he ceases to be one's husband. Each time he came I had to love him anew, but when he was gone again, how could I keep loving him? For a long time I have been empty of love, a marrow plant without fruit."

Lying in the street, in the morning twilight, Jamshid could hear the bells of the camels coming into Shiraz with fruits and vegetables from the country. From all over the city, street after street, rang the dull, empty beating of their tin bells. It was a haunting sound. It made him think of Hassan the camel and of the trip on the desert, and beyond that his old empty life. He wanted so much to have a new life. He kept thinking of the widow, and of their lovemaking.

"Father-dog," a harsh voice cried. "Lying there in public with a growling hard-on!" Jamshid opened his eyes. It was full daylight. The construction workers were gone. A policeman was standing over him. Curse these flimsy pajamas, Jamshid thought, sitting up.

"The snake must learn to uncoil itself if it is to get into its hole," he said quoting the proverb. "Where are my mates?" he added, in feigned alarm. It wasn't the right word. "Allah save me, I have overslept!"

"I believe your *mates* . . ." the policeman said, stressing the word sarcastically, "have gone off to work." He pointed up the street. "There, where you can see that *other* crane . . ." The policeman went off chuckling at his witticism. Jamshid got up and walked toward the construction site. Up in the open second story he saw some workers huddled at a fire making tea. When the policeman was out of view he inquired of a kerosene-vendor the whereabouts of the nearest highway out of town.

"The Tehran road starts just over there," the man told him.

Why not? Jamshid thought. Where is it easier to lose yourself than in a great city?

When he reached the outskirts of Shiraz he sat down under some trees. He was uncertain what to do. As for walking all the way to Tehran, it was out of the question. And yet he was afraid to hitch a ride, lest the police had put out a warning about him. He ate his bread and cheese and considered his situation.

Once in a while a tank truck would roar by, throwing up clouds of dust. He watched them pass. Some part of him wanted to remain in this city, where he had learned it was possible to be happy. Perhaps he would never be able to come back. He would not see the widow again.

While Jamshid sat brooding, a little white auto-
mobile drew to a stop before the trees. A foreign man
got out and walked to the rear, where one of the tires
was flat. He was muttering in a foreign tongue. Had
the man been Iranian, Jamshid would have slung the
carpet over his shoulder and trudged off. But these foreigners, everyone knew, drove about the countryside
perfectly ignorant of the local murderers. They were
known to be somewhat dim-witted and untrust-
worthy, but the best of them were said to possess a
trace of charity. Probably due to their Christianity,
Jamshid reflected. He recalled the religious dramas he
had seen as a boy, in which an actor playing the part of
the foreigner said to the cruel Yazd, as they stood over
the body of the martyred Hassan, "Why did you kill
this man?" The foreigner had always put much re-
proach into the question.

Jamshid stepped out from the trees and watched the
tire-changing over the man's shoulder.

"Salaam alaikum," the foreigner said, without turning from his work.

"Salaam alaikum," Jamshid replied. The man rolled
the old wheel around to the front of the car. Jamshid
followed. The man looked up and spoke. It was a ludi-
crous sound, this foreign language. Jamshid wanted to
laugh. The fellow was idiot enough to think you could
stop your car way out in the middle of a foreign country and expect the first person who came along to
speak the same language as you.

The man spoke again, and this time Jamshid realized that the man was actually speaking Persian. It was
the peculiar accent that made it sound like a foreign

tongue. "Why are your roads covered all over with nails," the man said, "when all your houses are made of mud?" He had finished changing the tire. After he screwed on the hubcap, he fumbled in the back seat of the car and came out holding a camera.

"Stand over there, will you?" he said, pointing to the trees.

"What?" said Jamshid.

"Yes, stand over there, for just a minute. I'd like to take your picture."

Why not? Jamshid thought. "Only if you'll give me a ride to Tehran," he said, as a kind of joke.

"Good," the foreigner said. He was squinting and turning knobs on his machine. Yes, it's true, these foreigners can be kind, thought Jamshid. If rather simple-minded. Now the foreigner aimed the camera. "That's it," he said. "Closer to the tree. And don't look at me." Jamshid looked at the car, which seemed much larger now that it was, so to speak, part his. "And stop *smiling!*"

Chapter Seventeen

They spent the night in Isfahan, the foreigner in the TPP Hotel and Jamshid on the sidewalk. He had wandered awhile looking for a quiet stretch of sidewalk to sleep on. It was the night the shops stay open and the great promenade was crowded. Many women in western dresses were on the streets. It was even possible to see couples strolling together. This air of freedom did not displease Jamshid. Rather he began to like Isfahan, and to imagine that one day he and the widow might come here and stroll down the promenade like the others.

As he lay on the carpet he thought of her. He could not deny that, according to all law and custom, it was wrong to have made love to her so soon after breaking to her the news of Ali's death. Yet nothing of what he and the widow had done seemed sinful. He felt surprised, and a little disappointed at the flimsiness of religion. He thought of Leyla. She seemed strange and unfamiliar to him. It seemed, for the first time, that he could forgive her—for anything, whatever it might be.

In the morning he went to the TPP Hotel and waited in the dining room for the foreigner to appear. The man looked ill-humored when he finally came in, but he seemed to brighten up on seeing Jamshid. They ate bread with butter and goat's cheese, and tea. The foreigner paid for it all. Jamshid had no scruples about allowing him to, though he protested several times. It was part of what one meant by 'foreigner', that the person had plenty of cash in his pockets.

They stopped the car now and then to photograph the sights. Jamshid found himself unable to tell what was a sight from what wasn't. If Jamshid thought his friend was going to snap a new gendarmerie, it turned out all he was after was the pigeons roosting inside its guardhouse. If he supposed the subject was going to be the new statue of the Shah, it was in reality the hairy tramp who sat hawking razor blades at its foot. So it went. A heap of rubble, then a Pepsi-Cola display, then some ugly fellow smoking a waterpipe.

The man drove very fast, and in a way Jamshid was relieved to see the outskirts of Tehran come into view. But he was also sad. It crossed his mind that a solution would be to emigrate to a foreign country. He asked the foreigner about it.

"Certainly," the man said, "but, of course, they would want you to have a trade."

"I do have a trade. I'm a carpet-repairer. I'm only temporarily out of work."

"Well, then, you must stop in to see the consul in your city, if there's one there. What city are you from?"

"Meshed," said Jamshid. Even as he spoke he regretted saying it. There was a moment's silence. The foreigner turned and looked at him, then looked back at the road. The look was grave and curious. The charm fled from everything, and Jamshid wanted to get out of the car.

"And of course," the man added, "they won't like it if you're a fugitive from justice."

"Look," Jamshid said, trying to control his panic, "here we are in Tehran. This very corner . . ."

"I'll get you a little closer to the center of town," the

foreigner said. "Anyway," he went on, "I read about your case in the papers. It's absolutely none of my business."

"God be with you," he said, when he had stopped the car.

"God be with you," Jamshid said.

Jamshid stood watching the tiny car weave away through the traffic. He was still shaking. How deeply he had been frightened. He who only a few days before had decided to give himself up voluntarily. He looked around at the people pushing by him. He had never seen so many at once, even at pilgrimage time in Meshed. Yes, it would be easy to lose oneself in crowds like these. And he was tired of traveling. He would be glad to lie low for a while. Afterwards he would go back to the widow. He had seen all the country he cared to see.

Cars and trucks were booming down the street, swerving and dodging and blasting their horns. In the old days the disorder would have made Jamshid's head grow sore. Now he did not mind it. Whatever it was that had happened, he wasn't exactly the same person.

He turned into a narrow street, on which he noticed there wasn't a woman in sight. Many of the men, he saw, were passing through a little gateway fringed by weeping willow trees. On the other side of the gateway there seemed to be another little street lined with weeping willows. It looked pleasant in there. Jamshid, too, walked through the gate. On the other side it was quiet. There were no automobiles at all, either parked or moving. And in the dense crowds many women mingled with the men. The place felt very strange to him, but he did not know why.

"Where am I?" Jamshid said, turning to a man.

"Where am I?" the fellow mimicked, a little drunkenly, in the Azerbaijani yokel's accent. "Tail of a scorpion! You're exactly where I am, in this crude paradise called the New City!" He spat. Where his spit landed Jamshid saw what he took to be the pale, sloughed skin of a serpent. He bent over to look at it more closely. It was an odd-looking thing. He poked it with his finger.

"Aiiiiiiieeee!" shrieked the yokel, so loudly a little crowd formed at once. "May my mother fry, this fellow's collecting used condoms!"

Chapter Eighteen

Jamshid ducked out of the cluster of jeering yokels and plunged into the moving crowd. As he walked along he noted with satisfaction that most of the men were from the country and almost as shabbily dressed as he was.

The street, paved in packed earth, was unlighted except for glaring naft-lanterns at the vendors' carts and green neon tubes over doorways and in shop windows. Under trees, in alleys, on doorsteps, he saw women of every sort, some with fair complexion, some dusky, some as broad as they were high, some as lean as planks, some dressed in billowing village pantaloons, some in bright cotton dresses, a few in tight-fitting embroidered trousers, others in the total modesty of black chaddor. Women sat or strolled like so many items on sale, while men streamed past, looking them over, sometimes stopping to talk, even to pat them like a chicken. Obscene phrases were offered like quotations from poems.

Was it here, in the New City, Jamshid wondered, that he was to start his new life? Yet he felt glad he had stumbled into this place. It excited him to be wandering here. Tomorrow he would look at the rest of Tehran and find himself a quarter in which to live. Tonight he would sightsee.

He passed a butcher shop where a skinned sheep hung in the night air. He stood at a shop window filled with gleaming new radios. He smelled the odors of a kebab stand and saw steam rising from an elaborately decorated beet stand. He saw a strong man demonstrating weight-lifting, and a darvish holding a live snake and haranguing a small crowd. It gave him a jolt when he went by a theatre entrance and heard the barker crying, "Come in! come in! See the poor brick-layer lay the rich man's daughter . . ."

The street came up against a high brick wall. Jamshid turned down an alley. This also ended at a wall. After further exploration he understood that the New City was in fact a city within a city. It consisted of a few streets and a connecting network of alleys entirely walled off from the rest of Tehran. The gateway he had come in by was the one by which he would have to go out. A policeman walked by. In a flash it came to Jamshid that this was no doubt the very worst spot in the city for a wanted man to wander in. Probably the police were studying all the faces, on the lookout for known criminals. . . . He cursed himself for having let the foreigner take photographs of him. What business did he have, going around trusting anybody he met? He wheeled and walked quietly back to the gate.

A long queue of men was waiting to get out. At the head of the line, under the willow boughs, he saw two policemen frisking everybody and looking at their papers. A pile of knives, razors, and pistols lay on a table. He inquired of a bystander what was going on.

"Five minutes ago," the man said, "a cement work-er horned in on somebody and got the stomach carved right out of him. They're hunting for the man who killed him."

"But listen," Jamshid said, feeling deep anxiety. "The man won't come out tonight. He'll lie low and come out tomorrow."

"Well, the police *are* stupid," the man said, "but not

so stupid as that. They'll be at the gate tomorrow too, and the next day. And even after they catch the killer they'll keep watching the gate for awhile. Of course, they'll only frisk you coming in, they'll give you back your weapons when you go out again. But they'll check papers both coming in and going out. It's to scare us into not killing anyone else for a little while."

Jamshid turned and walked slowly away. And then broke into a slow run. As he ran human shapes seemed to be blown out of his path. He ran more swiftly, noticing half-opened mouths, paralyzed smiles, suspended gestures, the carpet on his shoulder knocking against people, until at last he found himself alone in an alleyway. There was a door. He opened it. Something leapt up and he gasped in fright, but it was only a chicken. He stepped in and shut the door behind him.

In a little courtyard, he sat down by the pool. He was out of breath. Why, once again, had he been so afraid? He thought of the afternoon he had so calmly walked into the police station in Meshed, begging to be arrested. He thought of the numbness he had felt the day he was recognized in the coffee house near Yazd. So this is what it means to taste happiness. He put his hand into the pool. The lights floating in the water broke into pieces.

A fat, middle-aged woman appeared. "Salaam alaikum," she said.

"If you care to wait I will be able to offer you a nice innocent young girl. The next thing there is to a virgin. She has a gentleman visiting her just now, but in fifteen minutes . . . five, if you're rushed . . ."

"No," Jamshid said. "not at all, I'm not in any hur-

ry at all. Actually I like waiting, if it comes to that . . ."
The woman looked at him sharply.

In a little while a pudgy man, perhaps some kind of
government clerk, came out of the house. He lowered
his eyes and scurried past Jamshid.

"Your turn," the woman told him. "That door. At
the top of the stairs." Fearing she would put him out if
he hesitated or refused, Jamshid went up as he was bid.

The walls of the little room were decked with pictures of actresses and starlets, the Queen and the former queens, pin-up girls, local ladies, and others, hung
up indiscriminately together in the devotion to human
beauty. On the floor in the center of the room a candle
burned. Behind it, in its dim light, sat a chaddor-
wrapped girl. Behind her, in her shadow, was a mattress.

"Salaam alaikum," the girl said, "sit down." She
was young, and her voice reminded Jamshid of his
daughter's. He felt sorry for this girl and ashamed of
himself at being here.

"Just a smoke?" the girl said, "Or all night?"

"All night." She told him the price. Though it was
nearly all the money he had, he accepted without bargaining. When he handed her the money he saw by her
hand that she was very young.

"What's your name?" he asked.

"Goli," the girl said. "Now don't start asking questions. You'll have to pay more if you want conversa-
tion too." She began to undress.

"Incidentally," Jamshid said, averting his eyes as
she pulled her dress over her head, "I recently injured
myself. If you don't mind, my idea is for us just to sleep
side by side tonight." He was prepared to have the girl

curse him or laugh at him. She only shrugged.

"You remind me of my father anyway," she said, and, still dressed in her underwear, blew out the candle.

Chapter Nineteen

At noon the girl came in and shook him.

"Get up you lazy ass-picker," she said. "A customer's here, and you're crapped out right in my place of work." She spoke roughly. Jamshid saw that she was rather pretty. She had a scar down one cheek.

"I would like tea," Jamshid said, hoping to postpone his eviction.

"You'll get pee-water," she said, "if you don't get out of here." She pushed him to the stairway and half shoved him down the stairs. The man for whom he had been thrown out of bed stood beside the pool foolishly smiling. His lips sagged, and there were sores around his mouth.

Lucky this degenerate didn't come first, Jamshid thought. I would have caught one of his diseases merely off the sheets. A samovar boiled in the corner of the garden and Jamshid made himself tea. He leaned against the tree, put a few chunks of sugar into the little glass, poured some tea into his saucer, and sat contentedly slupping it. He looked at his new surroundings, the slime-filled pool, the sunlight, the willow limbs at which a goat was chewing, the chickens pecking hopelessly in the dust, the yellow cat pressing along his ankle. His sense of oppression had lifted. He did not want to go out again into those police-ridden streets. If he could just manage not to get thrown out of this little oasis for a few days, until the surveillance of the gate had lifted, he might yet escape.

He heard a rustling noise and a moan. In the doorway of the downstairs room a hag was dragging herself into the light. As she clawed forward she kept collapsing and moaning. She held her noseless face turned toward Jamshid. He saw at once she was out of her head. He went to her and took her under the arms, to help her come forward into the light. But she twisted in his grasp and one of her hands flashed up. He dropped her and leapt back pressing his hand to his face where her fingernails had cut him. The middle-aged woman of the night before trotted from the kitchen and set about berating and scolding the old creature. Soon the girl appeared too. The two of them carted the hag back into the darkness.

"She can't bear it if a man touches her," Goli said. "She likes to scratch them. Don't think about it. She's going to die soon, so we can't be angry with her, can we?" She drew boiling water from the samovar and set about cleaning the scratch.

"What's she got?" Jamshid asked.

"Syphilis. In every house in the New City there's one or two like her. Hags of her kind haven't any place to go, and we think it's our duty to take care of them. One day we ourselves might need a home. We all get old, don't you agree?" Jamshid looked at her but she dropped her eyes.

She continued to swab his cut. Her recent client came out buttoning his trousers. "God be with you, woman," he said, and spat into the pool. Goli did not answer but she made an obscene gesture after him as he went out the gate.

"Aiiiiiiieee," came a scream of torment from the

room into which the hag had been carried. Jamshid sat bolt upright.

"What's that?" he said hoarsely.

"Oh," said the girl, "it's only the hag. She's got these old bottles of medicine, that she pours on her sores."

Chapter Twenty

All afternoon Jamshid sat under the willow tree. He drank tea and chatted with Goli's clients as they awaited their turn. The chickens knocked their heads on the earth in search of grain. Goldfishes dozed in the green muck; a few floated belly up. The yellow cat studied them. The goat slept. Every so often the hag moaned. It was miserable enough, as oases went, Jamshid decided, but he prayed he would not be put out.

The madame, Effat, came over and talked with him. She was too fat and old for the trade, and only on the very busiest nights could she still get a customer. Over her face were wrinkles formed by a smile she seldom had occasion to use any more.

"So you're traveling?" she asked Jamshid.

"I wanted to see the country," he said.

"Well, sweetie, you're seeing it. It makes you skinny, though, seeing the country." She squeezed Jamshid's arms and thighs. "Traveling may be pleasant, but it doesn't do you a bit of good. I've a son who travels, and he's not a mescal fatter than you are."

That she had a son startled Jamshid. What sort of an upbringing could a prostitute have given him? But then he thought of his own unlucky daughter.

"How many children do you have?"

"Oh, about a dozen," Effat said. "I didn't mean to have children, of course, but they kept on coming. All kinds. I sent them to the poorhouse and I pay their keep. I even have a foreign one with yellow hair and blue eyes. I don't care for him, though. I find him a little insipid. My favorite is my eldest boy, a love-child, you could say, who's very dark with beautiful dark eyes that drive the women crazy. He's the one who travels, and he's as skinny as you . . ." As she rambled on Jamshid kept an eye on the door through which came the hag's moans. He grew depressed. Everyone's life seemed so hopeless.

"Travel!" Effat went on. "How I would like to travel! I want to go to Russia, for instance. I have a brother there. He's a doctor. One day I went to the Russian Embassy and told them I wanted to go to Russia and visit him. They said, 'Give us three photographs of yourself and we'll send them to your brother. If he admits you're his sister we'll fly you to Russia free.' Of course they'd shoot me in Russia if they found out I was a whore. Still, who cares? But I never got my pictures. I've grown so fat and ugly I don't think my brother would recognize me . . . I used to be pretty, you know. . . . The girls you see around here aren't real whores at all. They're mostly just a bunch of sluts. I used to be a true whore. I had a straight neck, see, like this, and slender shoulders, and nice firm breasts, and the thickest thighs you've ever seen, and a smile that could knock your eyes out they said. Look what's left." Tears were in her eyes as she tore off her blouse. The flesh was sagging from her in large loose folds, like so many rice bags. Her long breasts drooped low. She showed Jamshid the blue serpent tattooed on her arm from shoulder to elbow. "Isn't it ugly!" she exclaimed. "I would never have had it done, but I fell for a handsome tattoo artist. I gave him everything, and all he

gave me in return were these horrible snakes. I'm afraid of snakes as it is, never mind having them on my
arms. But I'm getting rid of them." She turned and
showed him the other arm. "See." Instead of a snake
there were thick red welts. "I put acid on it. It's supposed to heal up . . . though it's been two months . . .
God help me . . . that acid-peddler was a sweet-talker
too, if you want to know . . ." She shook her head.
"Yes," she took up the former subject, "The point is to
get there. They might shoot me. They might hang me.
They might shove red-hot irons up my ass. So what?
And who knows, maybe it would turn out they do
have whores in Russia . . ."

Jamshid laughed, but he felt pity for this half-naked,
tear-soaked creature wallowing in absurd dreams.

A young man stuck his head in at the gate. He
glanced about and then stepped in. He was Goli's
'beau', a greasy fellow who sang in nightclubs. Effat
made him tea, and as he waited for Goli to appear he
chatted with Jamshid.

"I used to sing in a nice place on Ferdowsi," he told
him, "a smart cafe where the rich women go and
drink. I'd buy them whisky when they sat with me,
and before I knew it I was bankrupt. Now I sing in a
filthy little dive on Naderi. When a woman comes in
she pays her own tab. But the women who come in are
poor as I am, and ugly as so many cans of kerosene. I
can tell you it's no life at all." He sipped his tea. "Of
course," he went on, "I might, you know, find a rich
one . . . who will sweeten life . . ."

Goli appeared and the 'beau' brightened up. He led
her to a corner garden. There placing the tip of his little

finger on his front teeth and fixing his eyes on the roof-
tops, he sang to her in a warbling falsetto. He went
into an intricate set of yodels, the tip of his little finger
still resting on his teeth. Then he led Goli into the
house. He made an exaggerated bow as she passed
through the door before him. Picking his nose, he followed.

"These days," said Effat, "if you try to be choosy
you end up with nobody."

Chapter Twenty-one

After the 'beau', looking bedraggled from his visit, had gone his way the government pharmacist arrived. He wore a striped suit and had octagonal, rimless glasses. He carried a fat black plastic satchel. His face was large and cheerful.

"Goli," the pharmacist said, looking at Effat.

"I'm Goli," Goli said.

"Goli, my dear," he said. "I'm afraid I've a bit of bad news to tell you." He slipped his arm around her in a fatherly way. His hand came to rest on her buttock. You've got yourself a little minor condition . . ."

"Condition? What condition?" Goli cried, slapping his hand away.

"Ah, my dear, I'm afraid it's a touch of syphilis . . ."

"Liar!" Goli said. "I wouldn't touch any of your rotten diseases with a mop-handle! Get out of here and stop annoying healthy women!"

"Now don't get hysterical," the pharmacist said. "Blood samples don't lie. If you saw your blood under a microscope you'd die of fright. It's crammed full of horrible bugs and germs. The wonder is you don't feel them creeping up and down your veins right this minute." He rummaged in his satchel and brought forth a great sheet of paper, which he handed to her. "Here. Go to the hospital tomorrow and take this with you." He turned away. "Filthy child," he muttered, half under his breath. Goli broke into tears. Jamshid jumped to his feet.

"That's no way to talk," he blurted out weakly. As the pharmacist turned to reply, Effat sprang to the attack.

"Mother-slut!" she shouted, "Get out of here!" The pharmacist fell back under her fury, turned, and made for the door with what dignity he had. But Effat was not going to let him escape so easily. She leapt after him, goosing him into a trot. "Where's his asshole?" she screamed, goosing him again. "I don't believe he's got one!" She let him have it once more, as the man scooted out.

"That silly little fart," Effat laughed, "trying to scare a healthy girl. Here, Goli, have a glass of tea." Goli sat down next to Jamshid.

"I'll turn into an old hag, just like Mehre," Goli said, weeping. "It'll eat up my nice face and make me crazy . . ."

"Hush," said Effat. "These days they take care of those things like magic. They stick your buttocks full of needles and in a week you're good as new. In my time, now, it was something else again." Effat launched into lurid histories about chancres, lesions, pustules, hair-loss, speechlessness, blindness and insanity, and about equally hideous cures. Not at all comforted, Goli wept on Jamshid's shoulder.

"Don't cry," Jamshid said. "Look, why not sing me a song instead? I love songs." He spoke to her as if she were a little girl. He felt a surge of tenderness toward her. She snuffled and looked up at him with puffy eyes. "I can't sing," she whimpered. "I smoke too much and it ruined my voice."

"Come on, one little song."

"All right," she said, and managed a smile, "just one, if you'll give me a cigarette."

"I'll give you a dozen," Jamshid said, laughing. He went out to fetch some.

The night before there had seemed to be an excitement and boisterous life in these streets. Now, by daylight, Jamshid saw only cold-eyed desolate men and obscene, humiliated women, and slime, and urine puddles, and ditches with used condoms in them.

At the cigarette stall the condoms, wrapped in silverfoil, and arranged in neat rows, looked to Jamshid exactly like the chocolate wafers he and Varoosh used to buy as children. Suddenly Jamshid felt dizzy. He had to get out, even if it meant he would be captured and die.

He put the cigarettes and matches in his pocket and made his way to the gate. Nobody seemed to be guarding it and he stepped forward eagerly. But behind some willow leaves he glimpsed a patch of wooly blue cloth. His willingness to die vanished. As he walked away he forced himself not to break into a run. Had they noticed his abrupt turning away? He could almost hear a hue and cry starting up behind him. When he reached the courtyard he slammed the door and threw the bolt.

"What's the matter, Jamshid?" Goli said, noticing how he was puffing.

"It's nothing. It's only an old illness," he said. "It makes me short of breath sometimes." He gave Goli a cigarette and lit one himself. It made his head spin, but he kept on smoking.

"Jamshid," Goli said, "do you want me to sing you a song in Persian or in Kurdi?" The girl's voice seemed to come to him from far away. He tried to concentrate.

"In Persian," he said.

"Are you absolutely sure? Kurdish songs, you know, are so much prettier."

"All right, then, in Kurdi." He felt the girl's warmth, and it cheered him up. At the same time it made him feel wistful, because she so resembled Leyla. And how, he wondered, was Leyla making her living without him? For the first time he understood that ordinary girls, no more wicked than anyone else, could become prostitutes. Previously he had believed that prostitutes were human fiends and should be destroyed like vipers or wolves. It was strange, too, that he felt closer to this prostitute he had met last night than he had been to his own daughter.

"That's too bad," Goli said, "because I don't know Kurdi." She giggled. Jamshid laughed too. He put his arm around her and gave her a hug.

Now a loud rattle came at the door. "Police," a voice cried, "Open up!" Jamshid jumped to his feet.

"I'm not here," he whispered.

"What?"

"I'm not here. I beg of you."

"Walk on my eyes," Goli said. She touched Jamshid's hand and he ran up the stairs to her room.

The police, it turned out, had only come on the complaint of the pharmacist.

"And be sure to go to the hospital tomorrow, or we'll arrest you for that too. And note well, under no circumstances are you to indulge your appetites or do business in the meantime. As for you," they said to Effat, "the next time you insult a servant of the government, you will find yourself in jail."

"We will leave the door locked," Effat said when

Jamshid had come out of hiding. "Goli is on vacation anyway, and these days nobody goes in for me. You must stay here," she told Jamshid, "until the gate is free again. Put your carpet there under the willow."

"Indulge your appetites . . ." Goli kept muttering angrily.

After dinner Jamshid sat against the garden wall. He had found his refuge. It was a horrible world, peopled with the degenerate, the sick, the used-up, but he was grateful for it. He liked Effat, and especially he liked Goli.

"Goli," he said, as Goli knelt by the pool to wash the dishes, "did you love your father very much when you were a little girl?"

"Yes," she said. "However, I hate him now. He made me a whore."

"What are you saying?" Jamshid answered sharply. "How can a father make his daughter into a whore?"

"My father ran off, and as soon as I could I whored around to earn money for the family."

"Listen," Jamshid said, hearing in his voice an anger he did not understand, "don't tell me he *made* you a whore! Why couldn't you have been a seamstress or a maid? You made yourself a whore and now you're looking for someone to blame."

The girl repeated firmly, "He made me a whore."

Chapter Twenty-two

It turned out that Goli had practically every sexual disease one can get, and she was ordered not to 'indulge her appetites' for a month. The news was a hard blow to Effat, for Goli was her only breadwinner. Effat made a few unlucky attempts to make up the loss. She offered herself to the men who came looking for Goli, and one night she went out soliciting in the streets. In the end she was obliged to 'rent' from another house a girl young and pretty enough to be the stand-in.

During this time Jamshid fell back into gloom. He knew he was a burden on these women. The longer he stayed the more his hopes began to seem as sleazy and unreal as those of everybody else. He felt uncertain even of the existence of the widow, as though he could have dreamed her. But whenever he went to the gate the police were there, checking everyone's papers.

Late one evening he happened to be sitting in the garden when Effat came in from her night of street-walking.

"Not a nibble," she laughed. "This blubber I use for bait!" She shook herself in such a way that all her flesh quivered and flapped. Even in her laments, even when the tears were cascading down her cheeks, Jamshid noticed, Effat remained somehow triumphant and invulnerable. In fact, he recalled, he had been thinking Ali was invulnerable at the very moment the old man was being killed. A wind started to whine at the edges of the garden. Effat, too, had been defeated out there. In the glow of the darkness he could only make out her forehead, her cheeks, her nose and the false shine of her lips.

"Tell me," he said. As he looked at her, her eyes grew visible a moment.

She said, "Out there, when they don't want you, they don't just say 'no.'"

Much later, as Jamshid was drinking tea under the willow branches, Goli's sore-lipped client stuck his head into the courtyard.

"Is Goli around?"

"Filthy germ-monger, get out of here!" Jamshid cried. Goli's sick, and you know why." The head withdrew quickly.

Effat looked from the house.

"Jamshid!" she cried. "What do you think you're doing? Stop chasing the customers away!"

"It was that ugly diseased one," Jamshid said. "The one with the sores all over him . . ."

"It's us who've got to get in bed with all those sores, not you. And never mind about the diseases. I've got a whole closet full of condoms for just such cases."

Jamshid sat unhappily under the tree. It was very easy, he saw, to have scruples on someone else's behalf. Perhaps, Jamshid thought, he could find the man and apologize; perhaps he could bring him back as a client for Effat.

Jamshid went out into the street but the crowd was so thick he gave it up and wandered over to the gate. As usual the police were there. A dozen or so men stood in line waiting to get out.

Poor Effat, Jamshid thought. Her error had been to

befriend him. A strange new pain now constricted his chest. It seemed to have five points, that dug into him in a kind of half circle. Was it for himself or for Effat and Goli? Or did it seize hold of him quite indifferently, as the painted hand print of the martyr grabs any wall whatsoever?

Jamshid noticed that a well-dressed man was walking abreast of him, glancing this way and that. The man seemed to give him one brief, quizzical look. He realized at once the man wanted a girl and was looking for someone to help him get a nice one. How grateful would Effat and Goli be, he thought, if he were able to persuade such a man to come back and take Effat. His gloom lifted. But before he could act the man had vanished.

Suddenly Jamshid glimpsed, in the glare of a kebab stand, his daughter Leyla dressed in a tight blue skirt. The glow of the fire lit her up a moment, then the dark smoke shrouded her. He plunged after her, but she, too, had disappeared.

He wandered in a frenzy of anxiety. He told himself he must have been mistaken. And yet he felt quite sure it had been she. He stared at the faces of all the women. He inquired at houses in the vicinity. After a while he glimpsed her again, this time wearing a chaddor. He ran up to her, but it was only an old hag, who spit at him when he seized her arm.

The third time he spotted her she was wearing the tight blue skirt again. He stepped in front of her and took her by the shoulders.

"Leyla!" he said. The girl looked at him, mildly astonished.

She said, "I'll bet I can screw just as good as your

Leyla, and I can let you have it very cheap, too, there in the shadows, standing up, if you're short of cash . . ."

Jamshid stood dumbstruck, staring at the mechanical, scarred face of this creature he had thought was his daughter. He dropped his hands. He stared again into her face, in the dim light, to be absolutely sure . . .

"Well, then," the girl said. She turned and disappeared.

Jamshid stood abashed. So then it wasn't his daughter. It couldn't be. He had looked her right in her face, hadn't he, and it was someone else's daughter. And yet, what did he know? Just because that blue-skirted girl wasn't Leyla, did that prove Leyla wasn't in the New City? One day or another he would see her soliciting somebody in an alleyway. His head began to throb. He could hardly see. The crowd swirled by, each face a blur. The tricks his eyes were playing! He might look his own daughter in the face, he thought, and fail to recognize her. That blue-skirted girl, for instance: why hadn't he looked at her *really* closely . . .?

When the streets had emptied, Jamshid went back and lay on his carpet in the courtyard. There was a crawling sensation at his crotch and in his neck and armpits, as there had been for several days. That night he had a nightmare in which he died and was put in the grave. Lying next to him was a corpse. He touched it and it said timidly, "Papa?"

Chapter Twenty-three

He was awakened by drizzling rain. It was the first rainfall of the year. The goat had come in under the tree too, and was sleeping next to him. He got up and went out into the streets. It was still dark, and the streets were quite deserted. The rain was falling very lightly. The dirt underfoot, trampled by so many footsteps, did not turn to mud but only grew a little slick.

As he walked past the dark houses his skull felt struck by a piece of iron. His head began ringing and aching. The other pain started up again at his chest, with sharp claws pressing toward his heart. He sat down in a doorway.

A few matches remained in his pocket. He felt anguish at the thought that they would get wet. He searched the ground. He found a bit of silverfoil and dried it as best he could. He wrapped it tightly around the matches, sealing the package well to make it waterproof. He was shivering.

He sat there most of the day. His shivering kept him from falling asleep. When at last it started to grow dark he got up and wandered through the quarter.

He saw a rich-looking man with a furled umbrella. He was strolling along and peering into doorways and alleys. This one, Jamshid observed, actually shone with the gold coins hidden all over him. Jamshid realized he could not interest someone like this man in so dowdy and plump a woman as Effat. But now he remembered this was the day the new girl was to start work.

With the pain gripping at his heart, he stepped forward and spoke.

"Excuse me." He was hardly able to get out these words. Yet the moment the words were uttered the pain lifted completely from his heart. "Excuse me, if it happens you're looking for a pretty girl . . ." He felt the inner, almost invincible strength of one who knows he is living the decisive moment. "I believe I can be of service . . ." The rich man stopped and turned to face him. "She's pretty . . . I could say beautiful . . ." He felt now as if a poem were about to spring from his lips. "A pure light dancing over the ground . . . ground full of bones . . ." Swinging with both hands, the man slammed his umbrella across Jamshid's face.

"Dirty pimp!" the man cried. Jamshid clutched at his face. The man stood staring at him, as if waiting for him to fall dead. Jamshid stared back . . . he noticed now the hooded eyes . . . the wide mouth. . . . Suddenly the expression on the face twisted into a grimace of horror . . . and the man vanished.

"Goli, run for the pharmacist!" Effat said, when Jamshid staggered into the courtyard. "He's just down the alley suctioning the last drops of honest blood out of poor Simeen. Somebody's hit Jamshid with a sword. Who did it?" Effat asked, as Goli ran out.

Those eyes . . . the mouth. . . . What else could account for that look of horror? If it *had* been Varoosh, what kind of man would break open someone's face just for being a pimp?

"I don't know," Jamshid said, suddenly seeing himself standing over the dead body of the mullah, "just somebody, a stranger."

Jamshid watched the hag who crouched in the doorway.

As the pharmacist—a different one—applied the bandage, he said, "Look at her! Some phony darvish talked her into buying a whole case of his 'Syphilis Potion'! In reality it's surplus rat poison. It was sold off cheap because the rats couldn't stand to go near it. It only burns her sores and keeps them infected. You can't take it away from her, though, or she'll rip you to pieces. She'd be better off if she'd drink it."

Jamshid wanted to ask the pharmacist about the sores that seemed to be appearing on his loins and thighs, but just then Mehre started crawling toward him.

"Get away, filthy crone," the pharmacist said. He quickly packed his black satchel and walked out.

Jamshid had not remembered to take Ali's old carpet in. It lay soaked in mud under the tree. It seemed the earth was actually absorbing it. He threw himself down on the rectangle where it lay. Pain flashed at his crotch again. He wondered if he had caught something just from touching Goli—or, in the sterile dust at Takhte Jamshid, had he made love with the mad woman in his sleep—and passed on her germs to the widow, keeping, to be sure, plenty for himself? He had not meant to cause very much harm in the world, he thought. But what he had meant seemed to have no relation to anything. He lay there groaning.

"Jamshid!" Effat cried. "Why have you thrown yourself in the mud? You've gone crazy too! Get in here. I'm putting you in with the girl tonight, on account of the rain. By the way, she's pretty, and even younger than Goli. I've told her to be good to you, if you should feel inclined. . . . Nothing's a better cure for sadness."

She spoke cheerfully. But Jamshid could see in her eyes she was troubled. "Jamshid," she said, at the foot of the stairs, "I've only learned one thing in my life." Jamshid turned. "It's that nothing matters."

"Nothing?" said Jamshid. *"Nothing?"* Effat smiled broadly.

"Nothing at all."

Chapter Twenty-four

Jamshid could hear the girl breathing across the room. In the New City he had felt desire only in imagining the widow. That promise on the horizon of a new beginning, however faintly it glowed—and never so faintly as now—was his tie to another life, a second world, and it put a barrier—perhaps mostly of pity—between him and these other women, who had only this one. Now, in this darkness which seemed to consist of the breaths, in and out, of an unknown girl across the room, the barrier suddenly vanished. He felt come over him an intense sexual longing.

He raised himself on an elbow, and looked in the girl's direction. The room was completely dark. It was a little like that darkness in Shiraz in which he had awaited the widow. As if the darkness itself were some kind of candlelight. He looked around him. Though it was totally dark, he felt he could see the photographs of beautiful women that were pasted all over the invisible walls.

He crossed the room. Kneeling at the girl's bedside, he heard the huge, passionate gasps of her body clamoring for air. It gasped with the ruthless will of an infant sucking at the breast. It was funny, he thought, how at night a person clings savagely to a life that, in the daytime, he only wants to throw away.

He could smell the girl's odor, bright and bewildering. With his hand he touched the smooth, hot skin of her arm. Sharp pains wriggled through his loins. He drew his hand away. And yet possibly it wasn't his disease that was hurting him, but the pain of desire. He reached out and touched her again.

Her breathing seemed to grow slightly deeper. He could not tell if she were awake or asleep. Surely asleep. And yet her nipples rose under his fingertips, and when he touched her belly it seemed to cave in a little under the caress.

"Ah, it's you," the girl said, waking suddenly, "the old man Effat said to be good to. That's fine with me. She says you're nice. Come in with me." Jamshid slid under her blanket. He moved his hand over the mound of hair. The gash between the thighs was wet and open. He opened it wide with his hand. The odor flared, like a dropped bottle of perfume.

He moved on top of her and thrust apart the loose thighs and pushed in. As he put his arms around her he felt on her back several tiny welts. Effat had shown him the little bumps on her own back where men had stubbed out their cigarettes. . . . He seemed to hear her sob. If so the sound had come from a great distance, a small cry from far down a street, heard at the moment a motor starts up and drowns it out. Some last, useless appeal. Her mouth kissed him back, her pelvis tipped up to meet him, she came alive down the length of her body. . . . They moved slowly . . . now more quickly, as a river gradually finds its bed deepening . . .

Jamshid lay looking up at the darkness. He felt no joy or peace. He remembered his disease. He felt only apprehension. Beside him the girl gave a low sigh. The sound caught in his mind. It had a familiar tone. . . . He abruptly dropped this idea. Yet his heart started to beat fast. . . . Now that he thought about it, there had been something so familiar in her voice. He did not dare speak, in case it was true. He put his hand out and felt her face. As he felt her he could see her. Yes. The eyebrows . . . the forehead . . . the cheekbones just so . . . the nose, exactly . . . the lips . . . chin. . . . He got to his feet and snatched up his clothes and plunged half falling down the stairs.

"Nothing?" he gasped, *"nothing?"*

He thought he would vomit but retched uselessly.

If only he could die. And as he was wishing to die he heard the sound of snoring—two snores—one deep-throated, made of groans and harsh warbles, one a high, empty rattle—now coming in alternating step like a thing with a limp, now one overtaking the other, now joined in sisterly unison. He stared swollen-eyed at the mud. The pains started up again in his crotch, first in crawling flashes, now as if actual fires burned in him. Tears poured down his face. The snores drew apart once more, and the high rattle resonated in Jamshid's mind. He realized he did know how to die.

He looked in at the open door. Effat was tossing under her huge tremors. Mehre lay trembling and shaking. Goli was heaped in a stiff and silent bundle in the corner. He stepped in. The snoring grew louder. Goli suddenly started up a wheezing, gasping snore. As Jamshid tiptoed toward Mehre's bed the noise continued to increase. It was like a jungle at night. He knelt now at the hag's bedside. Reaching across, he groped down in the space between the wall and the bed. His hand struck a bottle and knocked it against another with a little clang. He withdrew his hand and froze. All the snores stopped at once.

One by one, they resumed. He groped again for the

bottle. The noise of the snores seemed to grow louder. It was as if the sounds had slid over some last edge of the human world. The room filled with deep, throaty noises of animal suffering. A breath gurgled like a new baby as it went in, and death-rattled as it went out. There arose a great seething, tearing, sucking noise, of an enormous mouth gobbling compulsively at life itself.

Jamshid touched a bottle. As he snatched it up, a claw tore at his arm and another grappled at his belly. . . . He wrenched himself from the hag's clutches and stumbled out the door.

In the courtyard, he unscrewed the cap and tipped the jar to drink. Nothing flowed. He held it up to the light. In the bottom of the jar lay something caked and pink. He smelled it. Face powder, a century old. He hurled the jar at the pool.

Now Jamshid saw the hag was dragging herself toward him, and he ran into the street. He kept running until he came to the gate, that passage back to the world. He wished only to throw himself at a policeman and beg him to shoot him on the spot. But he could not see a policeman. He stopped and looked about. As he stood there a man walked past him and continued to walk through the gate and out the other side. Jamshid was astonished. The gate was not guarded. He was free.

Chapter Twenty-five

Frayed branches hung all about him. Ahead, in the open world, it was no longer raining. Against the pale sky the corners, angles, and rectangular markings of the buildings began to define themselves. Any minute the whole place was going to blaze up in gorgeous color and to fill with symmetrical trees and great emblematic birds. And if donkeys walking out there with mincing, effeminate tread were to happen to cry out, their cries would be bright and lucid, like shepherds' pipes, or young girls' laughter.

He looked across the threshold at the world where his new life would begin. But how could he step out there? Wasn't he kin to those filthy, dark beings which, in his shop in Meshed, he had so desperately tried to hide and do away with? He did not know if he had the right to pass through. He stood still, trying to keep from staggering.

A girl was walking down the street behind him. He turned and looked at her. For an instant he thought it must be Leyla. He couldn't be sure. He studied her face as she moved past him. It made him draw in his breath. What was it that caused the radiance in her features? It was a light coming from paradise. Tears stung his eyes. He guessed that it was, just as likely, a light reflected up from some fire of dread or disgust in her breast.

From a garden somewhere in the New City he heard a cock crowing. Perhaps, he thought, it is a bird of paradise, the original one, crowing in the mud. Jamshid sat down in a doorway. He stared at the empty gate. He took out his little package of matches and opened it. He struck one against the wooden door. Was it the match, or the wood, that was damp? He struck another. This did not light either. The world was dark, and we who inhabit it are also dark. He struck another, and another. He wanted now, more than anything, to see. Then he struck the last match. It flared a shrill, yellow, upwardly blackening flame. He got up and passed through the gate under the distant pale sky of early morning.

Afterword

In 1959 I spent six months in Iran as lecturer at the University of Tehran. Because of my feelings for the country, I arranged to stay on another six months as a journalist, writing a weekly article about Iran for the English-language edition of a Tehran newspaper. In preparing these pieces I wandered about the country quite a lot, sometimes with friends who knew Iran very well, more often alone, and with the five hundred words of Farsi I had managed to acquire, I was able to get along pretty well. The Japanese writer Makoto Oda titled his book about his travels, *I Saw As Much As I Could;* that is what I tried to do while in Iran.

This note is simply to acknowledge the obvious — which is that while I saw as much as I could, alas I wasn't able to see everything. In a regular novel, one expects a description of surface life — which *Black Light* may provide. But one also expects a certain understanding of the social fabric. For me, as a foreigner who spent only a total of twelve months in Iran, it was impossible to know much about the inner workings of that ancient, complex, tradition-ruled, abruptly modernizing country. But I did not intend *Black Light* to be a naturalistic novel; rather I had in mind to write a book that would be closer to a fable than to a novel and thus could not pretend to depict an actual society.

In preparing the book for re-publication after its first appearance fourteen years ago, I made a great many small revisions throughout. Each revision seemed a matter of style, yet the cumulative effect has been, perhaps, to change perceptibly the entire mood of the book.

Galway Kinnell

Design by David Bullen
Typeset in Mergenthaler Sabon
by Robert Sibley
Printed by Thomson-Shore
on acid-free paper